Road To Remember

Backroad Benefactor book 2

Riley Dawson

Contents

While this is a work of fiction, and the stories are all a product of my brain, along with some collaboration with a person I have come to know over the last several months. They are based somewhat in fact. The main character of this book is based on a real person, someone that I admire immensely. He faced his demons and came out on the other side. Since knowing him, I have seen him be more open and honest than many would be willing to be. He shares his story in hopes that he can help someone else find their way to a better place. He inspires me to want to do better and be better. He has given me the courage to write outside of my comfort zone and he has helped me see that there were certain people that would never make me a priority in their life, so they don't deserve to take up space in mine. So, while the situations and stories aren't real, the hero very much is. I know that he will say he's not a hero, but this is my book, and I say he is, so he can't argue. [] Thank you Kevin R Davis for everything you have become to me as a friend. Congratulations on over four years clean!

From Kevin R Davis-Model

My road to addiction started in my early thirties. I started having a lot of neck and upper back pain that continued to get worse and worse. For about 10 years, I did chiropractic, physical therapy, epidural injections, and nerve blocks. During that time, I was given some narcotics for pain, but the narcotics caused me to have severe stomach issues so I ended up looking for other drugs that would help relieve the pain.

I found that meth not only helped with the pain, but it made me feel so alive and productive. Eventually though, you need more and more of it, and you become less productive and can only focus on where your next high is going to come from.

Over the course of time, I had two neck surgeries, but by that point I was in full addiction, and my addiction told me that I was still in pain. I became a functioning addict for many years, but ultimately it started spiraling me down into a dark place. I was smoking and shooting meth on a daily basis.

I ended up homeless for about 6 months, crashing at friends, or sleeping in my car.

I eventually hit rock bottom when I was arrested for possession. I was face down on the ground, hands cuffed behind my back. I was locked up for 55 days. I thought my life was over, it was my worst nightmare, but little did I know, that was the best thing that could have happened to me. It caused me to finally face my issues and I couldn't hide it from the world any longer. It was what saved me. If it hadn't happened, I don't know that I would be alive today.

During those days, I was able to detox and able to do a lot of thinking about my life. I decided that I did want my life back, and I decided to do whatever it took to get there.

For once, my family knew about the secret life I had been living all those years. It felt very freeing to no longer be carrying that secret alone anymore. As part of my sentencing, I requested rehab. I was so ready to get my life back and I wanted to do whatever it took to get there. I was so tired of just existing, and I never wanted to go back to that life or go back to jail. When I was released from jail, I spent 3 months in rehab at Tuscaloosa VA Medical Center.

After rehab I decided to stay in Tuscaloosa, because I didn't know anyone there and I would have less temptations. Because I had not had sex without using for so many years, sex was my biggest trigger. I decided to remain celibate as part of my recovery and am still celibate as of today.

I also started putting a lot of my time and energy into the gym. It gave me a distraction and it made me feel good about myself again as well as transformed my body and looks.

I found a job and have remained employed. I also was approached online by Golden Czermak of FuriousFotog about doing a photo shoot. That photo shoot really changed my life. It gave me even more reason to get in my best shape yet and helped tremendously with my self-esteem. It opened up so many doors for me in the modeling industry and I have had such an amazing success as a book cover model. Golden has motivated me to keep rising and to be a positive force to help others do the same.

I've also developed a very large social media following, where I am able to share my story of recovery and am hopefully able to inspire others and show them that it is possible to quit, and you can have an amazing life. It's never too late to start over. I started my recovery right before my 50th birthday, and my fifties have been my best yet!

I feel so thankful to all the people, including my family who have helped me get to where I am today. I have so much to be thankful for and I hope that I can inspire and help others who are dealing with something similar. Blessings truly do come back to you when you do for others and the joy that you get from seeing those people rise is absolutely amazing.

If you are struggling with thinking that it's not worth trying for a better life, I'm telling you that it is so worth it. You probably think it's not fun, and it's scary to give up the life that you've been living for so long. It may seem impossible at the moment, you may think that nothing will change, so why even try. Well, it isn't fun, and it is scary, and it doesn't happen overnight and you most likely will have setbacks, but it definitely can happen for you.

And to me, it's scarier to think about what would happen if you don't ever change. Make a plan and stick to it. Don't do it alone and tell others so that you are accountable and have a support system. If you need advice, find someone like me who has been there, they obviously have no room to judge.

This part of the message is not for people with an addiction though, it is for the people who love and care for someone with addiction.

I like most, did not get the help I needed until I hit rock bottom.

Rock bottom will be different for every individual. If you continue to enable someone with an addiction, you are keeping them from hitting rock bottom, and that could keep them from ever getting the help that they need.

I know that cutting someone off feels like you are abandoning them when they need you the most, but it might be the thing that actually saves their life. Helping them find help is great if they want it, but they have to be ready to make a change.

Introduction

I've had enough.

After thirty years of living and working in a fishbowl, I'm done. More power to those who can keep on going, but this guy is burnt out.

You can call it a midlife crisis, chickening out, losing my mojo. I don't mind, because I don't really care. You see, I've done some re-evaluating of my life and I'm just not happy.

So, I've taken some photography courses on the side, got my financial ducks in a row, and now I'm going to travel around this big old country of ours to see what it has to offer.

And I'm doing it old school.

None of this GPS rubbish. I've got an atlas, a compass and a sense of adventure a mile wide. (Ok, I might have packed some extra underwear, but you get the gist). I'm going to visit the places people say they want to see before they die, and I'm going to capture snapshots of what I see there for those who'll never make it.

I'm Ray. Ray Hawthorne. Nice to meet you.

It's the end of the corporate road for me. Time to start a new journey.

The story that follows is the second stop on my journey.

Prologue

Ray had been driving for about four hours when he decided it was time to find a place to grab a bite to eat and get out and stretch his legs. He wasn't far from his next destination, the Grand Canyon. He would ask at the restaurant if there were any hotels or bed and breakfasts nearby. He ate his meal and while he was standing at the cash register waiting for someone to come and take his payment, he noticed a small bulletin board. There was a sign that said, 'Free Room and Board in exchange for handyman.' There was an address and a phone number. Something in Ray told him this was his next stop. He wasn't a carpenter or anything, but he had done most of his own upkeep and repair on his home over the years. He would at least stop by and see what all they were wanting in exchange for the room and board.

The waitress had given him directions to the address on the paper. He was watching the house numbers looking for the right one, when he spotted what looked to be a man at least ninety years old on a ladder. It looked like he was trying to clean his gutters. There was no way Ray wasn't going to try to intervene. His conscience wouldn't let him. He could just imagine the nightmares he would have picturing this old man falling off that ladder and breaking something or worse. He parked on the side of the road and approached the man, he didn't want to startle him too badly because that might make him fall too, but he wasn't sure how to get his attention. Nature took care of that for him when he stepped on a twig he hadn't noticed on the ground, and it snapped under his weight. The old man turned to see what had caused the sound.

"Hi." Ray began. "Are you by chance the one looking for a handyman?"

"I am" the man said. "Are you looking for work?"

"Well, I guess that kind of depends." Ray said. "I'm not a carpenter or plumber or anything, but I have done most of the upkeep on my house in the past."

"I don't need anyone with too many skills." the man said as he came down from the ladder. He was very slow and unsteady. Ray was tempted to reach out and help balance the man, but he wasn't sure how the man would feel about a stranger taking his arm. "Mostly just cleaning the gutters, mowing the lawn. I got some boards that need replacing and some things that need painting. I would do it myself, but I'm not as young as I used to be, and my legs just ache sometimes."

Ray held out his hand and said "I'm Ray. I'd be glad to take a look and see if they are things that I think I can handle."

The other man shook his hand and said "I'm Dick, Dick Mitchell. You needing a place to stay, Ray?"

"I do." Ray admitted. "I'm going to be taking some pictures of the canyon and I need a place to land for a while. I'm not on any set schedule, so I can drive up and take pictures in between things you need me to do around here."

"Well, come on in then." the old man said. "I'll show you around."

Ray felt like maybe he had found his next adventure along the way. If he could help this man not have to be on a ladder again. He would gladly stay and do so.

Chapter One

Dick showed Ray the things he needed done around his house. None of them were overly difficult. Some might require a trip to the hardware store or a lumber yard, but there wasn't anything Ray didn't feel he could handle.

"I think it's all pretty straight forward." Ray said. "I'll work on the projects outside on good weather days and then we can prioritize the other things as to what is needed most. I can start on the gutters today since you have the ladder out there already."

"That sounds fine." the man agreed. "I will tell you though that I go every day at three o'clock to see my Millie. She eats her dinner better if I'm there. Then I come home and have my own dinner around six."

"That's fine." Ray agreed. "I'm flexible. I don't even mind helping get dinner around. I'm a fairly decent cook if it's simple fare."

"Oh, that's fine either way," Dick agreed. "I'm a simple man."

Ray wasn't really sure who Millie was and was hesitant to ask. He wondered if maybe the man's wife was in a nursing home. So, he asked a simple question, "Is Millie your wife?"

"Oh, yes, we've been married for sixty-seven years." the older man said with a smile. "She was only fourteen when we started dating. Her momma was so strict with me. She was such a young and pretty thing. She still is pretty."

"I'm sure she is." Ray said.

"You should go with me; she'd love to meet you." Dick said. "She loves to have people come and visit."

Ray was fine with going to a nursing home or wherever to meet this man's wife. He was sure that they were both lonely, having to be separated like they were. He could understand the man not wanting to give up his home and go into a facility himself, but it was obvious that the time he spent with his wife was precious to him. "Sure, I'd love to meet Millie."

"Oh, she'll be so happy to have you." Dick said. "I'm the only one that goes to see her every day, usually. Our daughter Beth goes sometimes, but it's hard for her. She'll love having someone new to talk to."

"Great, why don't I go out and work on that gutter for a while and then you can show me where I can clean up and change." Ray said. Ray wasn't sure if it was hard for Beth to visit because it was difficult to see her mother sickly or in a home, or if it she worked and had a family so her time and ability was more scarce.

"Sure, sure." Dick said. He sounded like Ray had made his day by being willing the help with things around the house and by being willing to go meet Millie.

Ray walked back out of the house and got up on the ladder to assess just what he would need to do the job. Fortunately, the leaf build-up wasn't really bad, it could be pulled out with his hands. He was just getting ready to head back down the ladder when he heard Dick approaching him.

"I brought out some work gloves and some garbage bags. I figured they might be useful." the man said.

Ray reached down and grabbed the items. He put the roll of garbage bags in the gutter, so it didn't roll away and then put the gloves on. "Thanks, I appreciate it. I set an alarm on my phone for two, so I'll be down in plenty of time to get cleaned up."

"Oh, you don't worry about how long you work, I'm not paying you, so you just go at your own pace." Dick said. "You get done whatever you get done, if it comes time for you to move on or go take pictures or whatever you don't pay no mind to what needs to be done here. I just appreciate anything you can do while you're staying."

Ray just nodded and thanked the man again. It really wouldn't take him much time to do the work that needed to be done. He didn't plan to leave until everything in the house was in working order and safe for the man himself. Dick went back inside, and Ray got to work on the gutters.

His alarm went off and he closed the bag he was working on filling and climbed down the ladder. He grabbed his main suitcase and went in to see where he could clean up and change. Dick showed him to a really nice room on the second floor with its own bathroom. "You just make yourself to home here. Whatever you find is yours to use."

"Thanks, I'll take a quick shower and get changed so we can go see Millie." Ray said.

"She's going to be so happy that you're coming with me." Dick said. He slowly made his way back down the stairs and went to get ready to go himself.

Ray had no idea what to expect when he met Millie, he wasn't sure if she would really be happy to have a stranger come to see her or not, but it seemed that Dick really wanted him to go so he would. He dressed in dress pants and a dress shirt, he wanted to look nice for his first impression on this woman. He had no idea why she was in the nursing home, but that didn't matter, he wanted her to think that her husband had a good man helping him with the things he needed done and he wanted her to not worry that some bum was taking advantage and living in their home free of charge.

When he got downstairs, he was happy that he had made the choice to dress up a little. Dick was wearing a sports jacket and slacks. Neither man had on a tie though. They walked out to the garage and Dick got into the driver's seat of the sedan. He started the car and backed out of the garage. "Millie doesn't always remember things or people, she always seems to remember me though, but she forgets others. She may think she knows you, or she may not. I always try to just go along with whatever makes her happy. The doctors and nurses say that's what's best for her. Unless it's something that she has to know, like taking a pill or something, it's best to just agree with what she thinks and act accordingly. She really doesn't say or do anything that's way off most of the time. A few times, she thought one of her nurses was her friend from school. Another time she thought the doctor was the minister from our church. We just play along; it makes her happier if we don't argue with it."

Ah, so she had Alzheimer's or some form of dementia. Ray didn't know a lot about the subject, but his own mom had had a little dementia just before she died. "Okay, I'll do whatever you need me to do. If I'm not making Millie happy, I'll gladly wait in the waiting room or the car, I want you to be able to have time for your visit."

"Oh, you'll make Millie happy." Dick promised. "Don't you worry about that, she loves people."

Ray wondered if Dick had a little bit of forgetfulness himself, considering how many times he said that Millie loved people, but it was probably to be expected of a man his age.

When they got to the facility, Ray was happy to see that it wasn't a sterile nursing home environment. It looked like maybe it had been a very small hospital a century ago, and while it still had tiled floors and things that would make it easier to keep clean and sanitized, it wasn't a cold uncaring environment. There were paintings on the walls, it was colorful but not gaudy. It was the kind of place he would want to be in when his time came for that.

As soon as they walked in, every person that saw them greeted Dick by name. It was obvious that he had come here often and was well liked by the staff. He smiled and greeted them too, he didn't say all of their names, but he made sure each of them got their own personal smile and head nod along with a hello or some other happy greeting. Ray had no doubt in his mind that Dick had come here every day since his wife had been admitted so he could spend time with her. He had never gotten to see his parents growing old together so much in love. This made his heart happy.

When they walked into one of the rooms, Ray's heart felt even lighter. This room had a personal touch. There were photos and knickknacks all around the room. It didn't have a cluttered feel, it felt like home. Dick walked over to where his wife was sitting in a recliner.

"Hello, Millie" he greeted her and leaned in to give her a kiss. "I brought someone with me today." He said moving aside slightly so that Millie could see who was behind him.

"Oh, you've brought Daniel." she said with pure joy.

Ray wasn't sure who Daniel was, but he had done a little reading up on Alzheimer's when his mom first started to show the signs of it. The one thing that he had gathered from his reading and what Dick had told him, was that it was often best to just let the person believe what they thought as fact. It would upset them if you tried to correct them or tell them they were wrong, they may even feel like it made them a bad person or had misbehaved if you debated with them. If their assumption wasn't going to hurt them or anyone else, it was best to just let it go and go along with them. Ray just smiled, not knowing who Daniel was, he wasn't sure what to say or do to seem like Daniel, but he wasn't going to be the one to tell her he wasn't that person. He would leave it up to Dick to correct her or not, whichever he chose, Ray was okay with it.

Dick seemed a little puzzled as to what to say or how to react. His Millie thought that he had brought their son Daniel with him to visit. Daniel had died in an accident several years ago, but Millie wouldn't always remember that. Some days, it seemed like she remembered some of their history, and other days, it seemed like she knew nothing before a few second ago. He always felt thankful that she seemed to always know who he was, but he also knew that might not last much longer. He knew that his wife didn't have much time left on this earth and he wanted her time to be happy. Already there were days where some foods were difficult for her. There were days that she didn't do much more than sit in her chair. Other days she had the strength to go to the cafeteria for a meal or two. She was always happier when she did because she truly did love people. But the staff took it one meal at a time. If she wasn't up to going to the dining room, they would bring her a tray, and someone would stay with her in case she needed any help with the meal. He didn't want to break her heart by telling her the man wasn't Daniel. Besides, she likely wouldn't even remember it the next time he came if she even remembered for as long as they were here for this visit. It could change from one moment to the next. Dick only knew that if he tried to correct her, it often made her feel like she was being scolded and she would cry and apologize for being wrong or being stupid. He looked at Ray to see if the other man seemed upset by what she had said. Ray just gave him a smile and a half nod letting him know that the ball was in his court, and he could say whatever he chose to Millie. Ray wasn't going to say anything himself.

"I told you I brought you company today, Millie. I knew you'd like to have a guest." Dick said.

"I always love it when Daniel comes." Millie said. "He visits me often."

"Of course." Dick agreed. "That's what a good son does, isn't it Millie?" He was hoping that his statement would give Ray some sort of explanation of who he was assumed to be.

"It is, and Daniel has always been such a good boy." Millie said. "Never a cause for concern, never got himself into trouble. He always got good grades in school. I've always been proud to be his mother." She smiled at Ray as she said the last part.

"Thanks." Ray said. He couldn't really call her mom, but he could act like the dutiful son and be kind to the old woman.

"Do you want to play dominoes today, Millie?" Dick asked. "You and I could be a team and see if we can beat him."

"If you want to." She said softly. "I want to do whatever you want to do."

"Oh, sure, Millie," Dick said, "I want to play dominoes is your favorite game." He went to a cabinet and pulled out a tin full of brightly colored dominoes. They would be easy to play with, even for a child, because if you couldn't count the dots, you could still coordinate the colors and play the right tile. He rolled a table over in front of Millie's chair and helped her to put the recliner upright. It was a lift chair with buttons, but he told her which button to use to go in the right direction. When she was upright, he told her to let go, so she didn't keep rising too high.

He placed the table right in front of her and pulled up a chair. He pointed to another chair that Ray could move to the other side of the table. When Dick sat down, his foot must have bumped Millie because she sort of grunted and said, "Oh, you kicked me!"

Ray knew there was no way that felt like an actual kick. Dick's foot didn't move that fast or that hard to have made it hurt, so apparently, the woman was overly sensitive to things like that. Dick immediately apologized and leaned over to give Millie a kiss. "I'm sorry, Millie, that was clumsy of me. Can you forgive me?" he asked.

"Of course I can. I love you, but please be more careful." She admonished.

"I will, Millie, I'll try." He pulled his chair closer so that he could sit right next to his wife, and Ray found a folding chair in the corner and pulled it up to the other side of the table. He was careful to keep his feet far away from Millie's.

Dick turned the tin of dominoes upside down and tried to dump them out without making too much noise. They were some sort of ceramic, though, so there was still quite a bit of a crashing sound. He began flipping the dominoes and spreading them, so Ray helped him make sure that they were all face down and no two were on top of each other. It had been years since Ray had played any sort of board game or table game like this one. But he was going to give it his best shot. It seemed to mean a lot to both of them.

Ray heard Millie tapping her nails on the table to get Dick's attention. When he looked at her, she pointed to her hair and quietly asked, "does this look okay?▯

"You look fine Millie." Dick stated. "Now, we need to pick seven of them, Millie. Do you want to pick them?"

Millie started picking out tiles. When she had six, Dick said, "That's only six Millie, we need seven."

"Okay." Millie said, but she didn't make any effort to pick up another tile, so Dick took one and put it with the others. He tipped them up so that he and Millie could both see them. Ray sat his up too.

Ray had the highest double, so he placed the first tile. Dick pointed to a tile and said, "That one can go on there Millie." She picked up the tile he had designated it and sat it next to Ray's. They played in turn until Millie tried to place a tile along the side of the other dominoes sitting in a row. "No, we can't play along the sides, Millie. We can only play on an end." The man was so patient with his wife and although he had to correct her often about which tiles would work and which ones wouldn't and where she could put them, he never seemed to get frustrated with her or say anything in a harsh or corrective manner.

Ray had never been married, he hadn't really ever been in love, but he could tell that Dick loved Millie more than anything in the world. It must have been so hard to watch his wife deteriorate the way she had.

They played several games not really keeping score other than how many wins and losses they had. They didn't count the points the way the game was generally played. They were just putting the tiles away when a young man wearing scrubs came in with a tray of food. "Hey, Millie, dinner's here. I figured you'd want to eat it with your handsome husband here."

"And my son, don't forget my son Daniel. He's such a good boy to come and see his momma." Millie beamed.

The man looked at Ray a little puzzled and Ray just softly shook his head in the negative.

"Oh, no, of course not, Millie." the man said. "I'd never forget your son." He smiled as he set the tray on the table in front of Millie.

Dick helped her cut her food and even put some on the fork when she struggled. Several times, she started to complain that she didn't want to eat this or that, but Dick pleaded with her and kept encouraging her to take her bites. "They won't bring you your dessert if you don't eat enough Millie. Desert is only for good girls who eat all their food."

At first, Ray had thought it sounded odd that Dick had referred to her as a girl, but as he watched them, he could see where Millie had become almost childlike in a lot of ways. She only cleared her plate because of his encouragement. When she complained that she didn't like something or something didn't taste right, Dick had told her that it was good, she should try it. Finally, after a lot of debate and even more encouragement, the meal was mostly eaten. Dick got up and pressed a button beside the bed. Ray assumed it was something similar to a nurse call button. When Dick went back to sit by his wife, Ray heard her again softly ask "Does this look alright?" pointing to her hair. Again, Dick told her she looked fine.

A few minutes later, the same man in scrubs walked in and said, "You did a good job of clearing your plate Millie, so just for you, I have a cupcake." He placed a brightly decorated cupcake in front of her and removed the food tray from the room.

Ray needed to use the bathroom, so he excused himself to go down the hall to find the public restrooms.

On his way down the hall, he saw the man that had brought Millie her tray. "Hey, thanks for playing along back there." he said to the man. "I'm actually just a handyman that's helping out around their house, but I have heard that you aren't supposed to correct people with dementia unless it's something they really need to try to understand, like medications or whatever. So, when she called me her son, I didn't agree or disagree. I hope that's okay."

"It's perfectly fine, sir." he said. "We all do the same. Our patients here vary in cognitive and memory level and we all just do our best to do what makes them happy. None of us would have told you to do otherwise. If it makes Millie happy to think you are her son, then there's no harm in that at all. I didn't even know she had a son. I've met her daughter on several occasions."

"I don't really know anything about the son, but if you haven't met him, I would think he doesn't live nearby. At least I hope that's his only reason for not coming to visit his mother." Ray said. "How long has Millie been here?"

"Oh, it's been close to a year now I think."

"I've done some reading about Alzheimer's, but I really don't know much. But I believe that the prognosis isn't good."

"No it never is with Alzheimer's, although some live with it for years and some pass quickly. The disease affects the brain and that in turn effects the triggers the brain sends to other parts of the body. Some get to the point where they don't swallow properly. Some have difficulty with falling because they tend to shuffle.

It's one of those things that you can't predict. It effects different things in different ways. So far, Millie does fairly well with eating. She first came here because she broke her hip, and Dick just wasn't up to being able to care for her at his age and with his own health concerns. Alzheimer's affects the memory in everyone who has it, the rest of it is unpredictable. One never knows if the brain is going to send the trigger to swallow or not." He continued, "And if it doesn't, the patient can choke or aspirate. Alzheimer's itself doesn't kill anyone, it's not that kind of disease. The person will die of something that is caused by the brain not telling a body part to function properly or as a result of an illness or injury that no one even knew the person had because they don't know that they should tell someone. Pneumonia is one of the highest rated causes of death. The person doesn't swallow properly, they aspirate, they get fluid in the lungs, and it spirals from there."

"Other causes include heart disease, stroke, almost anything can cause death for them because they may not understand or report things. For example, if someone had chest pains today, but doesn't remember that tomorrow, they don't tell anyone, so it goes unnoticed and untreated. If it was reported, they could get treatment and likely live a long life with proper treatment, but if you don't remember or understand that, it goes untreated and is often only found postmortem. Honestly, almost anything can cause death for them because they don't tell anybody. If there aren't outward signs, something can be damaging them internally for a long period of time."

Ray couldn't imagine how hard it must be for Dick and for their daughter to know that this was the prognosis for Millie. "You said you've met her daughter?"

"Yeah, her name is Beth. She started out coming every day, she doesn't do that anymore. She still comes a couple of times a week though. I think it's hard for her because Millie doesn't know who she is at all anymore."

"That has to be hard." Ray said. "But she remembers the son, or at least thinks I'm him even though he doesn't come to visit at all." The man just shrugged as if he didn't understand it either. "Thanks for all of the information."

"No problem." The man walked away to get back to his duties and Ray went to find the restroom. By the time he got back to Millie's room, she was back in her bed and her television was on.

"I'm going to go home and have supper now Millie." Dick said. "I'll be here tomorrow." The man leaned down and gave her a kiss.

"You'll bring Daniel with you too, won't you?" she asked. She looked at Ray and said, "You'll come back tomorrow too won't you Daniel?"

"I'll try." he promised. He didn't mind visiting her, but the likelihood was that she wouldn't even remember that he had been here today and by tomorrow would wonder who he was if he came back to visit.

When they got back to the car, Dick said, "I want to thank you for not saying anything about not being Daniel. It would have upset my Millie if you had told her, you weren't him."

"That's no problem, I don't fully understand Alzheimer's, but I do know you said it's best to not correct things that don't really matter." Ray said.

"Well, I appreciate it just the same." the old man stated.

"Does Daniel come and visit? Maybe that's why she got confused." Ray asked.

"Daniel died twenty years ago." Dick said sadly.

"I'm very sorry to hear that."

"Millie said he was always a good boy, and that was true when he was young. Although he was an average student, not all A's like Millie said. But he was a good boy. When he turned twenty-one, he got in with the wrong crowd and started drinking and doing drugs. He never really did amount too much after that. He died in a car accident while driving impaired."

Ray didn't really know what to say to that. He could see that maybe Millie didn't want to remember the bad parts, so in her mind, she had kept him alive and pure. "When I went out to the bathroom, one of the nurses was telling me that Beth goes to visit a couple of times a week."

"She does, our daughter Beth." Dick said. "Now she was the straight-A student. She's a smart one. She comes over most days, not every day, but most. She goes to see Millie, but I think it's hard for her to do that. Millie doesn't remember her or thinks she's someone else and that's hard for Beth."

"I'm sure it would be." Ray agreed. "I think it's got to be a difficult disease for anyone's family to deal with."

They had arrived back at Dick's house, and he went in to start dinner. "I think it's a horrible thing." Dick said, as he walked away.

Chapter Two

The following morning, Ray got up and had a cup of coffee and a bowl of oatmeal with Dick before starting back on the gutters. He had found that the man wasn't really much of a cook, but he did basic things okay. That was fine with Ray. He didn't need fancy food as long as he could eat. He was fine with whatever. He put the ladder back up against the side of the house and headed up to finish the gutters. After he had been working for a couple of hours, he saw a car pull into the driveway. A woman got out. She appeared to be around his age. He had a feeling this might be Beth.

She noticed him on the ladder and came over to say hello. "You must be Ray." she said.

"I am, and I'm guessing you're Beth."

"I called my dad earlier, and he said he had someone doing some work around the house. I wanted to stop by and meet you."

Ray had a feeling that she had wanted to meet him because she was concerned about her father having someone staying in his home. She wanted to make sure Ray wasn't some lowlife trying to take advantage of an old man. He gave her credit for being willing to step in if it was a bad situation. He went back down the ladder. "Well, I'm a photographer of sorts. I retired from a large corporation and decided that I wanted to see the country. I bought some equipment and set out to take photographs of both national landmarks and the everyday people. I find that I enjoy getting a chance to know people and I'd rather stay in a boarding house or a situation like what I have here with your dad than to stay in some chain motel. I'm not a carpenter by any means, but what your dad needs done is fairly simple upkeep, really. So, I saw his flyer in the diner, and I figured I'd stop by and see what was needed. I'll be honest, when I pulled up, he was on that ladder trying to clean the gutters and I had a flash of him falling off the ladder and breaking something so I was determined to try to do as much of the work as I could."

"I appreciate you getting him off of the ladder." Beth said, "I'm a little surprised you could, that man has some stubborn pride and doesn't want to admit that he's over ninety. He wants to do things like he did when he was young. I've tried to convince him to come stay with me or me move in here, but so far, he says he can manage. I can't force him, unless he gets worse. I understand him wanting his independence, but I worry about him."

"Well, I'll do my best to keep him off ladders for however long I'm here." Ray promised.

Dick came out of the house and said "Oh, Beth, you've met Ray. I'm so glad you stopped by so the two of you could get to know each other."

Beth had walked over and gave her father a hug and a kiss on the cheek. "Hi dad. Ray tells me you were up on the ladder when he got here."

"Oh, I was fine." Dick huffed. "I didn't fall."

"No, but you could have, and you know you don't want to break anything." Beth said. "You let Ray do the gutters and anything else that needs to be done for however long he's here."

"I will, I will" Dick said. Ray hoped he was telling the truth.

"Come inside and have a cup of coffee with us, Ray." Dick said.

Ray followed them inside and really enjoyed getting to know Beth. He could tell that she really loved her father and would dote on him if he would let her. After they had visited for a while, Beth said "Why don't I throw together something for lunch, since I'm here."

"You don't have to do that." Dick argued.

"I know I don't have to." Beth said with a wink, "I want to, I like doing things for you dad."

Ray was curious as to why they hadn't been able to come to an agreement on Beth staying with him, yes, the man was stubborn, but it would seem like it might keep him in his home longer.

It turned out that Beth was a really good cook. When she had said lunch, Ray had expected a sandwich or something similar. He hadn't expected the sandwich to be a grilled cheese with three different kinds of cheese and bacon. "This is really good." he told Beth.

"Thanks, but it's nothing special, just a grilled cheese sandwich." she said.

"That's a huge understatement." Ray said. "This is like gourmet grilled cheese.

"I enjoy cooking." Beth said with a shrug.

"Well, I better get back to the gutters or they'll never be cleaned." he said standing up. He took his plate and glass to the sink and started to walk out the door.

"Don't forget we leave to go see Millie at three." Dick reminded him.

Ray wasn't sure how Beth was going to feel about him visiting her mother, so he said, "I'd be glad to stay and work on things if you and Beth want to go without me."

"Oh, nonsense, you can both go." Dick said.

Ray looked at Beth to see if he could get a read on what she was thinking of that suggestion, but she just shrugged as if she didn't care either way.

"Okay, I'll be back inside in time to get cleaned up." Ray said. This cleaning the gutters job was going to take a lot longer than it should if he visited Millie every day and had coffee and a long lunch. But he got back to work, he had a little over an hour to make as much progress as he could.

When he went into the house, Dick was down the hall and Beth was sitting in the living room. "Beth, I just wanted to tell you, when we visited yesterday, Millie thought I was Daniel. I don't know if she will continue to think that or if it was a one time thing. But I wanted you to be prepared in case it happens again."

"That figures." Beth said. "Thanks for letting me know."

Ray wasn't sure what she had meant by 'that figures', but he wasn't going to try to get the answer from her. He was sure she had suffered lots of hurts with her mother's condition. He went upstairs to get dressed.

Beth had driven separately so that she could go home after the visit. When they got to the nursing home, they walked in together. As soon as they were all in the door, Millie said "Oh, Daniel, you've brought a girl, is this your wife?"

Ray had absolutely no idea what to say or do but he looked at Dick for an answer.

"No, Millie, that's your daughter, Beth." Dick reminded her.

"I don't have a daughter." Millie said, "I only have a son, Daniel."

Ray could see the hurt in Beth's eyes, and he thought she might tear out of the room, but she didn't. He would give her credit for her strength in this situation.

"You do have a daughter, mom." Beth stated. "You just don't remember sometimes, but that's okay." Ray could tell that it wasn't okay, but Beth had come to accept that her mom might never remember her again.

The visit went pretty much the same as it had the day before, dominoes, and then Dick helped Millie eat her dinner. Twice during her meal, she had asked Dick if her hair looked okay. It made Ray wonder if she had been a vain woman in her younger years, or at least one that had to be dressed up and looking perfect before she went anywhere or had company over. When she finished, Dick pushed the button again and this time, Millie was brought a slice of cake. Ray wished he could get a chance to talk to Beth, but he wasn't sure how to go about doing that. It might seem odd if someone who was basically a stranger said 'hey, let's go out for coffee'. But there were so many questions that he wished he had answers to. He could see that Dick loved Beth, he could tell that she loved her father, but there was something there that was making it so that they had a sort of wall between them.

He would have to ask leading questions when he had a chance and see what he could piece together. As they walked out of the facility that evening, his dilemma was solved for him.

"Ray, could I take you out to breakfast tomorrow morning?" Beth asked. "I'd like to welcome you to town and thank you for all you're doing for my dad."

"Sure, that would be great." Ray said.

"You can manage breakfast without Ray, right dad?" She was saying more than a 'you're not invited' statement than anything.

"Oh, sure. I manage just fine alone." Dick stated.

Beth just rolled her eyes a little but told Ray she would meet him at the diner at eight the following morning and got into her car.

"Beth seems really nice." Ray said on their ride home.

"She's a good girl." Dick said.

Dick let Ray help with dinner. He tried to say it wasn't necessary, but Ray had insisted. The man wasn't really much of a cook. Mostly just TV dinners, frozen meals and pot pies, things he could just put in the oven, and they would be done a short time later. This wasn't really a healthy way for the man to eat. But Ray supposed at ninety-one, he wasn't going to change his habits easily.

When they sat down to their food, Ray said "Beth sure can cook, can't she?"

"Oh, she's a wonderful cook." Dick agreed.

"She told me that she offered to move in here and help you with things. I'm surprised you don't let her." Ray said. "No offense, but you'd be eating healthier if you'd let her cook for you."

"I just don't want to be a burden." Dick began. "She has a husband, and kids and grandkids, she doesn't need to be bothering with an old man like me."

"I don't think she'd see it as a bother." Ray said.

"She won't say it is, but I know having to pick up and move in with me would upset her normal life. I can't do that to her." Dick stated.

Ray decided to drop the topic for now. But at least he had Dick's side of things to at least start a conversation with Beth the following morning. After he was finished eating, he said "I'm going to go take a look at those loose boards you told me about in the back room."

"You don't need to work so late in the day." Dick argued.

"Well, I didn't get much done today and I feel like I'm not earning my keep around here. And I'm going away for a little while in the morning, so I need to do something. I won't work late, but I at least want to assess the situation and see what it's going to take to fix it. I don't know if I'll need new boards or if I can work with the ones that are already there."

"Okay, suit yourself." Dick said. "I have lots of miscellaneous stuff in the garage, depending on what you figure out."

Ray put his dishes in the sink, he had noticed that the ones from the day before had been washed, most likely by Beth when she had taken care of the stuff from lunch. Dick said he didn't want his daughter to have to move in, but she was already doing a lot of what she would do if she lived here. She was just having to drive over every day to do it all. He made his way to the back room; it was kind of a mud room or something like that. It looked as if it hadn't been put to much use in recent years, maybe because of the boards that needed to be fixed. Although, with it only being Dick living in the house, he didn't really need a mud room. He didn't need much of the space he had. He could move into a smaller place and have less upkeep, but Ray was sure this house held a lot of memories for Dick. Memories of his wife and his children during the years when things were good for them. He could understand the man not wanting to leave as long as he was capable of staying. What he didn't seem to realize was that having Beth and her husband move in, just might lengthen his ability to stay.

Ray had a lot of questions for Beth. Her husband might even be able to help with some of the upkeep of the home. Not that Ray wasn't fine with doing it, but if Dick could see that his family could be self-sufficient and support each other in all kinds of ways, he might find that he didn't need a stranger living in his home. That would be fine with Ray. If Dick didn't need his help, he could easily find a hotel or someplace to stay while he took his photos.

Ray was happy to find that the boards didn't need replacing, they were in good shape, they just needed to be screwed down tighter. He made his way out to the garage. He hadn't really been in there before. He looked around and it looked like Dick had had a pretty decent work space to use when he had been up to it. There were even some craft type things that the man had likely made over the years. Some were finished, some were in various states of being worked on.

He found a bunch of old peanut butter jars filled with every type of nail and screw you could imagine. They were sorted by size and type. He found the jar that held the size that would work for tightening down the floorboards and went back inside. He stepped on each board and if it wiggled. He figured out where the weakness was and screwed it in more tightly. He had opted to use a regular screwdriver rather than something with power. He knew Dick would be going to bed soon, if he hadn't already and he didn't want to make noise to keep the man up. It took longer that way, but within a couple of hours, he felt satisfied that every board in the room was secure. He put the jar of screws back where he had found it and headed to bed. He would shower in the morning. It was getting late, and he wasn't sure how much noise Dick could sleep through.

He sent off a quick email to Hope, asking how Lance was doing and what was going on in the small town he had just left a few days before. He had really liked that town and the people he had met there, and Lance would always have a special place in his heart.

Maybe someday, when he had seen all that he wanted to see of the country, he might consider settling down there. It would be close enough to Los Angeles that he could go there if he wanted to visit old friends or if he wanted to have some unique foods from around the world. Los Angeles had just about everything you could imagine and he loved that aspect of it, but living in a big city just didn't hold any appeal for him anymore. But being only a short drive away from the city might be nice and he had definitely found fast friends in on his first stop. Although, he had a feeling that most small towns would be similarly welcoming.

Chapter Three

When Ray went downstairs the following morning, Dick was already up having a cup of coffee at the kitchen table. Ray didn't know what time the man got up, but he seemed to be an early riser. "You get up early Dick." he stated.

"I used to be the one that had to get to the office early to start the coffee for the day. I guess it just got ingrained in me. Although I grew up on a farm, so I've always gotten up early I guess."

"Well, I'm going to head down to the diner in a few minutes to meet Beth, but I'll be back and get to work on those gutters. I finished the back room last night though. So that's one thing off the list."

"Oh, that list is no rush. You take as long as you need on that." Dick said. "Enjoy your breakfast and send Beth my love."

Ray was pretty sure that Beth would be coming over at some point in the day, but he promised to send along the message.

When he arrived at the diner, Beth was already seated in a booth near the back corner. He made his way back there and accepted the cup of coffee the waitress offered him.

"I'm sure you have lots of questions, and I do too, but feel free to ask anything you want to know. I'll answer the best I can." Beth began, "But I'll warn you, a lot of the answers will have to do with the fact that my father is an independent and stubborn man."

"Well, why don't you start by telling me what you think I should know and if I have questions, I'll ask." Ray said.

"Okay, that's fair." Beth began. "Well, going way back, my parents had three babies. Only one lived. They were all boys. But they were advised to not try for more children. My dad came from a family of twelve and he had always wanted to have a big family. Most of his siblings had four or more children. Now, it wouldn't be an issue, but best I can figure from what I know is that mom has negative blood and dad has positive. Now they just give you a shot and everything's fine. Before they discovered Rhogram though, when Dan was about eight, they got the chance to adopt, and they chose me. I had been given up by my biological mother at birth. That's a whole other story for a different day because I have found my biological family, but it hasn't gone well. But I sometimes wonder if that's part of why my mom doesn't think she has a daughter. Either because she didn't actually birth me or because she knows that I found out who my real mother was. If I could go back and change things, I would."

They paused their conversation to place their orders and Ray interjected. "Still, it must be hard to hear your mom say she doesn't have a daughter."

"It kills me a little more inside every time I hear it, but I have to try to remind myself that she doesn't remember much of anyone or anything anymore. I'm just one of the casualties of her disease." Beth said.

"She hasn't ever forgotten your father, though?" Ray asked.

"Not so far, but we all know that day is probably not far off. I can't imagine what it will do to him if that happens." Beth said. "We've been fortunate that she's remained one of the people with Alzheimer's that's generally happy though. Some get combative and argumentative. My hope is that even if she does forget everyone, she still enjoys having visits and people around her. I think even if she didn't remember my dad, she would seem happy to see him and that would at least help ease some of the pain for him."

"But she remembers that she had a son. She just doesn't remember that he died." Ray said.

"Yeah, well, my brother was always her favorite. Everyone in the family knows that. You can ask anyone. I don't know if it was because he was the oldest, or the only child that survived or because he was a boy." Beth said. "I remember being introduced at family functions as their 'adopted daughter'. It was hard, but it was what it is, I guess."

"So, you always felt a little bit on the outside looking in?" Ray suggested.

"I did."

"Is that why you haven't moved in with your dad?" Ray asked.

Beth's face flared with either anger or frustration. "No, the reason I haven't moved in with my father is that he's a stubborn and independent man. I've offered numerous times, other than threatening to put him in a home, there's not much I can do to make him let me move in."

"If he wanted you to, you'd do it?" Ray asked, "What about your husband, is he okay with that?"

"He's totally onboard with the idea." Beth said. "He even offered to do a lot of what you're doing for my dad around the house, but my dad says he doesn't want to be a bother. If you have any idea of how to get my father to change his mind, I'm open to hearing it."

"I don't know if it would work, but it might be worth a try." Ray began. "But what if your husband just showed up and started helping me with the list Dick gave me of things that need to be done? I don't think that Dick would tell him he can't. At least not if I thank him for the help."

"I'm sure Tom would be glad to come and help. Like you said, it might not work, but anything is worth a try at this point." Beth agreed. Her eyes began to get misty and she said, "I know that people with Alzheimer's will eventually die from complications of the disease. And it's one of the things that no one can predict. I would really like to be there for my dad when that happens. I don't know that he will function after she passes. I think he'll give up on life himself. I hope I don't lose them both at the same time, but I'm fully aware that is what's likely to happen."

"Well, all you can do is do your best to be there for him." Ray consoled. "If he won't let you, you have to understand that's not on you. Just make sure you tell him you love him every time you see him. I learned the hard way that you never know when it will be the last time you see someone."

"You've lost a parent?" Beth asked.

"I lost my dad years ago in a divorce, but yes, he passed away a few years back. I regret that I still had hard feelings over the fact that he walked out on us and started a new family. He died without me ever having a chance to work things out with him. My mother died a little over a year before he did. She didn't have Alzheimer's, but she was starting to have memory issues. I tried to tell her that I loved her every time I saw her when I knew it was getting close to the end of her life, but I don't know if it registered with her or not."

Beth reached out and put her hand over Ray's, "She knew Ray, she may not have heard or understood the words towards the end, but she felt it every time you went to see her."

Ray gave a nod that he appreciated the sentiment of her words whether or not he was sure they were true.

"Do you have any siblings?" she asked.

"I have a half-brother; I've never met him. He was part of my dad's new family. When my dad walked out, he never looked back. It made me pretty bitter for a long time." Ray said, "But I've started thinking about looking him up some time. I've realized it wasn't his fault that our dad was an ass to my mom."

"You should Ray. I've come to realize lately that family is important." Beth said. "Especially as it starts to get smaller and smaller, you wish they were still here, and you question if you did the best you could while they were."

That was something Ray had been thinking a lot about. The only family he had left out there was his half-brother and a cousin. He thought maybe the cousin had kids and a wife, he wasn't sure, but he thought he had heard that at some point. He was already sort of stalking the brother on social media. He wanted to see if he could get an idea of who the man was before he made actual contact with him. The cousin would be easier, they hadn't seen each other in years, but they at least knew each other.

"One other thing that I'm curious about, your mom always asks at least two or three times if her hair looks okay." Ray began, "Was she a woman that put a lot of time into her appearance."

"That's the odd thing, she really didn't. I don't remember her ever wearing make-up or any of that. She got perms in her hair sometimes, but she never really pampered herself. I've wondered if it's a part of her feeling her own limitations but not understanding them. Like maybe she knows something about her isn't right, but she's not sure what, and that's her way of making sure she's still got something. I wish I knew a real answer, but I don't."

"So, she broke her hip and that was kind of where the downhill slide began?" Ray asked.

"Well, not completely." Beth began. "Before she broke her hip we had started to notice some things. One night I was there for dinner, and she put a large bowl on the table and announced that dinner was ready. It was pancake batter. She had followed the directions on the box to make the batter but had forgotten that it needed to be cooked."

"Everyday things were starting to slip her mind." Ray said.

"She was always so good with money. She had a knack for finances I guess, but I can remember when she started not being able to count her money anymore. She would start with one, two, four. She knew that wasn't right so she would stop, but she couldn't remember the way it was supposed to go. She would just hand the money to my dad and ask him to count it for her. There were a lot of things that he covered for her on. I took over some papers one day that I needed her to sign to renew her insurance and she couldn't remember how her name was spelled. My dad told her letter by letter and helped her make the right ones."

"And then she broke her hip?" Ray asked.

"She did and we were in the middle of a pandemic so no one could go and see her. She went from the hospital to the rehabilitation facility, but no one could visit. I honestly think that was what made her decline even faster. For a month, she didn't have any connection to anyone or anything she knew. Dad tried to bring her home, but she remembered even less than she had before she went in. A few months before she broke her hip, we had her evaluated and she was diagnosed with moderate to severe Alzheimer's. I think being there all alone made it go all the way to severe. Since she got released from the rehab facility, she doesn't know me much anymore. She doesn't know my husband or my children at all. She doesn't remember her own grandchildren or great-grandchildren. She always loved to have them come visit, but to her they were just children who she enjoyed watching as they played or whatever."

"That has to have been hard for all of you." Ray said. "I'm sure the young ones don't understand the change in their great grandma."

"No, but they've been troopers about it." Beth said.

"So you were adopted?" Ray asked.

"I was, I was given up at birth and I was adopted by the time I was just over three weeks old." Beth stated.

"Do you know anything about your biological family?"

"Well, it's had it's challenges." Beth began. "I found out I was adopted from a neighbor girl. I had inadvertently gotten her in trouble with her mother and she was mad at me. She told me that my real mother hadn't wanted me, in fact no one had wanted me, and she had dumped me along the side of the street. She said Dick and Millie had felt sorry for me and had taken me in, even though they really didn't want me either."

"That's horrid." Ray said.

"Yeah, well you know how kids can be. She was enough older than me that she knew I hadn't shown up in the usual way babies do." Beth began. "Anyway, I went running home crying my eyes out and my mom sat me down and told me the real story. They had always planned to tell me when they thought I was old enough to understand. It just happened sooner than they planned."

"Being told that way had to have left an impression." Ray said.

"Oh, it did." Beth said. "I think I've always felt like I'd better be the good girl, or I might get discarded again. Not that my parents ever did or said anything to make me feel that way. But I think it was just there in the back of my mind. I think that's a big part of why I made sure I got the best grades. I didn't skip school, I didn't try any drugs or alcohol or go to parties. I didn't want to be sent back."

"That makes sense." Ray agreed.

"My mom told me that my biological mother was only thirteen when she had me. That was a totally legitimate reason to have given me up." Beth said. "The thing was that I always thought that if I ever did try to find my mother, I'd be very cautious. I didn't want to barge into her life. I mean, who knew if she had gone on to get married and have kids, she may not have ever told them about the child she had when she was just a kid herself. My plan was if I found her, I would just write a letter and say 'hey, this is who I am.' Maybe tell her about my kids and my life and then give her the opportunity to decide if she wanted to reach out or not."

"That was a kind way of going about things." Ray said.

"I thought so. Anyway, just before my mom started having memory problems, I took those DNA tests, and they all started pointing me in the direction of two families. One had to have been my maternal side, and one had to be my paternal side. But there wasn't really any way to know for sure which was which because there were men and women in both. The more digging I did, the more confused I got. None of the women fit the age for having been thirteen when I was born. But as they say, DNA doesn't lie."

"So, how'd you figure it out?" Ray asked.

"A man from one family had married a woman from the other family. Odds were that they may have been my parents, or if not, they at least knew something most likely. They had gotten married about a year after I was born, so if it wasn't them, it was their siblings. They would have known if siblings had dated and might even know if any of them had a pregnancy. So, I wrote a letter to her. He had passed before I found them." Beth paused for a moment and then continued, "I did what I had always planned to do, even though there was no way the story about a thirteen-year-old was true. I wrote a very simple letter explaining how I had done DNA and who I had found that made me connect the dots, at least to the two families. I said that I believed that either she or one of her siblings was one of my parents. I gave her the information to be able to contact me if she so desired."

"And did she?" Ray asked.

"She did, almost immediately. And yes, she was my mother." Beth again paused for a minute. "She was excited to make contact and said she had looked for me for years. But things were sealed, and she couldn't be the one to open them., only I could."

"Did she tell you the true story since she obviously wasn't thirteen?" Ray queried.

"She did." Beth stated. "She was staying with her sister when she found out she was pregnant. She contacted my father, she said he was the only possibility. She told him she was pregnant, and he promised to come and marry her. He didn't show up though, so she decided to give me up."

"But they ended up together." Ray said puzzled.

"Yeah, after she signed the papers and I was born, she stayed with her sister for a while longer, but eventually went back to her hometown. She ran into my father, and they ended up back together. They got married and stayed together until he died in 2003."

"Did they have other children?" Ray asked.

"No, she was never able to have any more kids." Beth said.

"Do you have a relationship with her now?" Ray asked.

"Of sorts I guess." Beth said. "I've come to realize that she most likely had borderline personality disorder, so it's difficult at best. She always has these big ideas and makes promises and then backs out on them. She wants interaction, but when it's not as often or as in depth as she wants it, she tells me she no longer wants a relationship. Then she comes back several months later and wants to work things out, but none of it is ever her fault."

"Ah, yeah that would be tough." Ray agreed.

"She lives about five hours away, I was trying to co-ordinate a trip so we could meet half way and maybe spend a day together, me and my kids and grandkids. A few weeks later, I get a text telling me she had decided to terminate our relationship. Which was fine, if that's what she wanted, then so be it. But almost a year later, she tells me that I wasn't even willing to drive a few hours away, so I wasn't making an effort. She never realizes that she had told me the relationship was done so of course I didn't continue to plan to make a trip."

"I know someone like that, he's always willing to admit that it might have been a mistake, but then he goes on to explain why it wasn't his fault that it happened. Someone said something or did something that made it happen." Ray stated.

"Yeah, that's exactly it." Beth said. "She doesn't deny that she may have done something wrong, but there's always a caveat. It happened because of something that was out of her control. She over reacted, but now it's different."

"Its kind of like watching a dog chase its own tail sometimes." Ray said.

"That's it exactly." Beth said. "I've told her that I'm not opposed to having a relationship with her, but I can't keep dealing with what feels like rejection every time she decides she doesn't like something. She says it's not rejection, and I'm sure she doesn't mean for it to be, but that's still what it feels like to me. I think most adopted kids have that same feeling. Especially with how I found out about it as a child. My parents explained that it wasn't that way, but the words of that neighbor girl are still in there somewhere."

"I totally get that." Ray said. "When my dad walked out, it felt like a huge rejection to me. As I got older and more mature, I realize that it wasn't at all about him rejecting me as much as it was that he and my mom just couldn't be together anymore. But then he found another woman and started a new family and it was a kick in the gut. I'm only now coming to realize that I need to let go of that resentment. The man's dead, my feeling of being rejected and still sitting here licking my wounds about that isn't doing me any good. You need to look at who you are, not who she makes you feel like you are. You're a mom and a grandmother and really good daughter to the people that matter most in the world. I'm not saying that you should completely write off a relationship with you biological mother, but if she can't see that what she does hurts you, then maybe you need to take an even bigger step back and see if she puts in the work to try to understand how her actions make you feel."

"I know, it's difficult to know how to proceed. I don't want to not have a relationship with her but I can't have one the way things are now." Beth said.

"No, right now you have so much to focus on, if she can't see that, she's not seeing what you really need from her. If the focus has to stay on her for her to be happy then it's not a healthy situation." Ray said.

"I know, I guess I'm too much of a people pleaser, I don't like letting anyone down." Beth said quietly.

"I get that, but right now, you have to be focused on other things." Ray said. "If she wants to have a relationship that's healthy and supportive, then that's great, but if she can't do that then she may have to wait until you're able to change your focus a little bit."

They finished their breakfast, and both agreed to try to work together in Dick's best interest. Beth said she would be there in a couple of hours to spend some time with her dad and to fix his lunch. As Ray had suspected, she did it every day to make sure her dad had at least one good and healthy meal every day. They said, 'see you later' and each headed out of the small diner.

Ray was up on the ladder when Beth arrived again. He had the gutters almost completely done. This time though, she had a man with her, Ray assumed it was her husband, Tom. He got down off of the ladder to meet them.

"This is my husband, Tom." Beth began, "Tom this is Ray, the man I told you about."

The two men shook hands and Tom said, "Show me where I can be the best help."

"Well, none of it is going to take any real construction knowledge," Ray began. "It's mostly minor stuff. I have the gutters almost done. I already fixed the floorboards in the mud room. There's some painting that needs to be done inside. A few shingles that need replacing on the roof, and some siding that needs to be replaced or at the very least reattached."

"I'll go take a look at the siding and assess the situation. You're using the ladder, so the roof can wait until the gutters are done. Unless there's a leak problem and the roof is more important." Tom offered.

"I haven't seen any evidence of a leak, not that you get much rain here in Arizona, but the ceiling tiles don't show any sign of water getting through." Ray explained. "I think it's more of them looking like they need to be replaced before it goes that far."

"Okay, I'll go take a look at the siding then." Tom said. "Do you know if there is any extra siding around if any of the pieces can't be reused?"

"I think I saw a partial package in the garage." Ray said. "To be honest from what I can tell, there's a little bit of everything in that garage. So, look there before you go buy anything new."

"Will do." Tom said, walking away to make a trip around the house to assess the siding situation.

About an hour later, Beth called them into the house for lunch. When they were all seated, Ray made a point of saying, "Tom's really good with that siding. He's further than I could have been in the same amount of time. If I find out I have to move on before everything gets done, I'm sure Tom would be able to finish it all up for you."

Dick just looked up from his plate and nodded. They finished their lunch and the two men got back to work while Beth cleaned up the dishes and spent time with her father. Ray was tempted to tell Dick that he needed to run to town or something so that he didn't have time to go see Millie and then he would suggest that Beth go instead, but he wasn't sure how Beth would feel about that. He could tell that visiting her mother wasn't an easy thing for her to do and she might need to space them out to not let herself get too depressed about the whole thing. He didn't want to cause anyone more pain than they could handle, so he got ready to go with Dick at the appointed hour.

Millie complained that her dinner had no taste to it and insisted that Dick try a bite. "Oh, it's good Millie, I really like it." he said.

"Then you can eat it." Millie stated.

"No, Millie, this is the dinner they made for you. I'm not supposed to eat your food." Dick argued.

"Well, don't tell them." Millie said.

"No, Millie. You need to eat it, so you stay healthy. They won't bring you a desert if you don't eat it. Do you need me to cut it into smaller pieces for you?" he asked.

"Maybe Daniel wants it. If he's hungry, he can have it." Millie said, smiling at Ray.

"No, you need to eat it." Ray said. "I don't want you to miss getting your desert."

Millie wasn't thrilled about no one taking her up on the offer of her food, but she apparently resolved herself to eating it. She was all about getting that desert.

Before they left, Dick turned on the television. "Your shows are on Millie." He put on a game show and said, "You are always so good at these Millie, you know the answers before I could ever come up with them. Remember, you and Beth used to keep score on some of them. Beth won most of the time, but sometimes you beat her."

"I don't know who you are talking about." Millie said. "Who's Beth?"

"Your daughter, Millie." Dick said. "You know Beth, she was here yesterday to see you."

"I don't remember anyone like that." Millie said. She seemed to be getting more and more confused, so Dick just let the subject drop.

On the way back to Dick's house that evening, Ray decided to try to start the conversation about Beth and Tom moving in. "Dick, can you explain to my why you don't want your daughter and her husband to move in with you, beyond the fact that you don't want to be an inconvenience?"

Dick was quiet for a bit and Ray thought maybe the man was just going to ignore him completely, but finally, he spoke. "That's it for the most part. I don't want to be an inconvenience, I'm an old man, I don't have a lot longer on this earth. Tom and Beth, well, they have a life and after I'm gone, that life will go on. I don't want to pull them away from the things they enjoy just to take care of an old man."

"Well, it seems to me that they have shown you that they feel just the opposite." Ray began. "Beth comes over every day to make sure you have a good meal. She does the dishes and straightens things up. I would think it would be easier for her to do all that if she lived there rather than having to drive over for a few hours every day."

"But they have friends and things to do." Dick argued.

"Oh, I get it now." Ray said sarcastically. "You wouldn't let them have friends over to visit at your place and they wouldn't be allowed to go anywhere. That makes sense then, I can see why you don't want to have them move in, they'd become virtual prisoners in your home."

"That's not what I said." Dick countered.

"No, but it's how you make it sound." Ray said. "They want to move in to help you. They don't see it as giving up their lives or anything else, they see it as what kids do for their parents. And I think they see it as a way for you to be able to stay in your home longer. They don't want to see you go into a nursing home if you don't have to."

Dick was silent for the rest of the ride to his home. Ray could tell he was mulling a lot of things over in his mind and he wasn't going to say anything more, for now. The thing was, he was the one that could say these things, if he did them right, Dick might accept the idea. If he did it wrong, Dick might ask him to leave, and while that wasn't what he was hoping for, it wouldn't put him in a bind and it just might push Dick to have to let his family help him. He was going to talk to Beth about an idea he had.

After they had eaten a mostly silent dinner, Ray looked at his watch, it wasn't late, so he called her.

"Hello?" Beth said cautiously.

"Hi Beth, it's Ray." he said. "I have an idea that I wanted to run past you."

"Okay."

"I know that Tom said there are some pieces of siding that need to be dealt with by two people, I think we can get those taken care of tomorrow. But I'm thinking that I might go and do some photography the following day. I need to get the pictures, and Dick knows that's part of why I'm here. The thing is though, that maybe if Tom came and did some of the things on the list Dick gave me, your dad might think about letting Tom do the whole list rather than needing me to do it."

"It can't hurt to try." Beth said. "But I don't want you to think you'll be put out on the street if my dad ever does come to his senses and lets us help him."

"Oh, I'm not worried about that. I always find a place to land. I have no set schedule, so when I get the photos I want of the Grand Canyon, I can move on anyway and I do have the money for a hotel, I just thought that your dad needed help and I could use the opportunity for free room and board. I don't want to make it so that your dad thinks he doesn't need you and Tom."

"I think he thinks he doesn't need us living with him either way." Beth said.

"Well, I talked to him about that a little bit tonight, I may have ticked him off a bit." Ray began, "But a big part of it is that he feels like if you move in, you're giving up your own lives. He feels like he would be taking you away from spending time with your friends and family. I challenged him on that and at the moment, he's not really speaking to me much, but I felt it had to be done."

"I appreciate you trying, and I'm sure he'll get over being upset with you. He's just so stubborn." Beth stated.

"Well, I don't really have a horse in this race as they say, so I'm not opposed to being the one to push him. I mean I'd like to see what's best for him, so I do have an interest, but of everyone involved, I'm the one that can walk away from it all if he gets too upset with me." Ray explained.

"Thank you for trying at least, Ray." Beth said.

"Well, I'll keep working on it when I can, but I'll see you and Tom tomorrow so we can get that siding taken care of."

"Okay, sounds good." Beth replied. "Good night, Ray."

"Goodnight, Beth."

Chapter Four

Ray didn't tell Dick that he had called Beth until he was headed outside to start working for the day. "I'm going to head out and get things around, Tom should be here shortly to help me with the siding. There are some places he said need two sets of hands so that's what we're going to work on today."

"Okay." Dick said. He was still kind of quiet, Ray wasn't sure if he was still upset, or if he was actually thinking about what Ray had said to him and the truth of it all.

Ray was just getting out the tools and things when Beth and Tom pulled into the driveway. He and Tom got started on figuring out the siding while Beth went inside to spend time with her dad.

When they went in for lunch, Ray decided to tell Dick that he was going to be going away for a while the next day. "Dick, I really need to head up to the canyon tomorrow. I've got to get started on some pictures."

"Oh, sure, that's fine." Dick said. "The work around here can wait."

"Well, actually, I was talking to Tom, and he knows a lot more than I do about most of the things on that list. Apparently, when he was in high school, he did some construction work. I asked him if he could take care of some of the things that I'm not sure my skills are capable of."

"That's fine," Dick began, "But you don't have to tie yourself up with it Tom. If you have other things you need to do, my stuff can wait."

"Nope, I have all the time in the world." Tom said. "Actually, I enjoy tinkering with things like this so it will give me a chance to do some of what I love."

"If it's not a bother." Dick said.

"No bother at all." Tom replied.

"I can come with him and help you get caught up on some of the laundry and housework." Beth offered.

Dick just shrugged his shoulders like he wasn't going to argue, but they didn't have to go to all that trouble for him.

"I'm not sure I'll be back in time to go see Millie." Ray said.

"She'll be disappointed to not see you." Dick began, "but she'll be fine."

Ray wasn't so sure she would be disappointed. She may not really even notice or remember, but he wasn't going to say that to Dick.

"I was planning to go see mom tomorrow anyway, so I'll just go along with you and then we can all come back and have supper together." Beth said.

"You really don't have to go to all that trouble for me." Dick stated.

Beth stood up and went to hug her father, "It's no trouble dad. It's what family does for each other. You and mom took care of me when I was little. It's my turn to pay some of that back by helping you."

Dick didn't say anything more either way. He wasn't going to fight it, but he also wasn't ready to admit that he needed the help either.

Ray and Tom were able to get the siding that needed two people done and there were just small areas that still needed some work. Tom could handle those on his own.

When they visited Millie that night, she just couldn't or wouldn't eat what they brought her for dinner. She kept saying that it had no flavor, and that she didn't like it. No matter how much Dick tried to bribe her with dessert, she wouldn't eat. Dick pressed a button on the intercom near the door and asked, "My Millie doesn't like her dinner. Would it be possible for her to have a sandwich or something else so that she earns her desert?"

"Of course, someone will bring one shortly." the voice on the intercom said.

A few minutes later, someone came in with what appeared to be a peanut butter and jelly sandwich, and Millie ate that so that she could have her desert.

"Beth and Tom are coming with me tomorrow, Millie." Dick said.

"I don't know who they are."

"You do, Millie," he began. "Beth is our daughter and Tom is her husband."

"Beth is your daughter?" she asked.

"She's our daughter." Dick corrected.

"I don't have a daughter." Millie stated.

Every time she said that it hurt Ray's heart for Beth. Even though she had been logical about it and said she knew it was the disease talking, Ray couldn't help but think that it really must hurt to hear that and know that her own mother didn't remember her. His own mother had forgotten things, but she had never forgotten him. Honestly, a lot of people probably wouldn't blame Beth if she decided that she couldn't handle visiting her mother.

"Well, I'm bringing Beth and her husband Tom with me tomorrow, you'll know them when you see them."

he stated. The thing was though that they both knew that she may very well not remember them at all.

"And Daniel, you're bringing Daniel." Millie said.

"He has things he has to do tomorrow, Millie." Dick explained. "He can't come tomorrow."

"Oh, that's too bad." Millie said sadly. "I like it so much when he comes to see me."

Ray felt a little bit of guilt at the woman's comment, but he had to remind himself that the goal here was to help this family find ways to bond and be there for each other and as much as it was difficult for him to disappoint anyone, Millie's illness made it very possible that she wouldn't even know he hadn't come.

They went home that evening and Ray wanted to at least make sure that Dick understood why he was going to miss seeing Millie. "I know Millie wishes I would come with you tomorrow, but I really do have to get these pictures started."

"Oh, no, it's fine, you don't worry about that at all." Dick said. "Millie doesn't always understand things, but she'll be okay."

"Okay, I shouldn't be out late, I just want to catch the sun and the shadows at various times of the day." Ray stated. "But don't wait on me for dinner. I'll grab something on my way back."

"Suit yourself." Dick said.

"Maybe the three of you can go to the diner for supper tomorrow night. It might be nice to go out with Beth and her husband." Ray suggested.

"I just might do that." Dick agreed. "It's a nice way to pay Beth back for all the meals she cooks for me."

"I wasn't meaning it that way, Dick." Ray said. "I'm sure Beth doesn't need to be paid back for any of what she does for you. She does it because she cares."

Dick didn't really say anything more, so Ray dropped the subject.

The following day, Ray headed out of the house early. He knew that Tom and Beth would be there before too late in the day. He had a very productive day, hot but productive. He had driven to a few different locations along the canyon and taken photos with the sun high and with it starting to go down. He had taken shots from the top and some from the bottom. He was going to send them off tonight or in the morning to see if there were any other shots his friend thought would be good for a magazine or whatever. He was going to stay in the area at least until Dick's fix it list was completed or the old man finally gave in and let his daughter and son-in-law move in with him. Either way, he was going to be here long enough for his friend to request another photoshoot or two.

When Ray got back to Dick's house, Beth and her husband were still there. He greeted them, but he could tell something was wrong, so he gave a puzzled look toward Beth.

"My mom is starting to have trouble swallowing sometimes." she said. "They're talking about maybe putting her on a soft food diet or a liquid diet to see if those things go down easier."

She didn't add the part that everyone in the room already knew. This was the next step in the progression of the Alzheimer's not sending signals to the brain.

"They say that she can't swallow the solids, but the liquids are easier to aspirate, so they're considering soft foods for a while. But they want our input. We have to let them know tomorrow." Beth stated.

Ray could tell that this information was coming close to devastating Dick. If his wife couldn't eat, or risked aspirating every time she did, it most likely wouldn't be much longer before she would get pneumonia or something similar and may not survive the illness. He had no words to say, this wasn't his decision to make. "Well, I'm sure that you will make the decision that you feel is best for Millie. I think it's one of those things were there isn't a right or a wrong answer. Most medical things are like that, you do what you hope is best for the person and that's all you can do."

"Thank you, Ray." Beth said.

"You're welcome, I've had a long day in the sun, I'm going to head upstairs and take a shower." Ray said. "I'll leave you to your family discussion."

He headed upstairs for the night. It was a long while later that he saw the headlights of the car pulling out. He didn't envy them on any of what they were having to do.

When Ray got up the following morning, he could tell that Dick was feeling defeated by the news from the night before. He was quiet and retrospective. He had a few photos laying on the kitchen table. Photos of him and Millie in their younger days from what Ray could tell. He didn't want to interrupt the man, so he didn't speak, he just went about getting some oatmeal and coffee.

"This April would be sixty-eight years since Millie and I got married." Dick said. "We didn't have money for a honeymoon. We went to visit my brother and his wife. They had a few kids by then, so it wasn't much of a vacation, but we were just so happy to be married, we didn't really care."

"I'm sure it was great." Ray said.

"You know, when Millie first asked her mom if she could go out with me, her mother said no." Dick began. "I had a few brothers that were older than me and her mom thought one of them was me. They had kids; her mom told her she couldn't date a married man with kids. It took some explaining for her mom to figure out that I wasn't one of them."

Ray smiled, "Mothers can be protective that way."

"And there was one time that my Millie had a date with another man, he had pulled into the driveway to pick her up and walked up to the back door of her house. I didn't have a date scheduled with her, but I didn't care, I walked up to the front door and asked her out while that other guy was knocking on the back door. You know who took her out that night?" Dick asked.

"I'll bet it was you." Ray said.

"Darn right it was." Dick said. "That other boy was so mad, but, my Millie, she knew that she was going to be mine someday. There was no sense in wasting time going out with other boys anymore."

"Well, when you know, you know." Ray said. "If you're falling for someone, there's no sense in pretending that anyone else has a chance."

"That's what Millie and I thought too." Dick said. "We waited until after she finished school to get married. But it wasn't long after. I didn't want to wait longer than I had to."

Ray smiled and said, "Well, it seems like it worked out well, you've been married for a long time."

There was a long pause before Dick spoke again. When he did, there were tears in his eyes. "What am I going to do without her Ray? She's been my whole life for so long that I don't know what it's like to not have her."

"I know, Dick." Ray said consolingly, "but, you've still got Beth and her kids and her grandkids. That's why I think it might be a good idea to let Beth and Tom move in with you. It's less lonely that way. And, if you did have a problem like a fall or something, they would be here to help you. From what I can tell, Tom's pretty good with the maintenance of the house and fixing the things that need fixing."

"I know, I'm sure he probably could." Dick said, "I don't know, it just feels like I give up my independence if I let anyone move in."

"They're family though." Ray said. "And I don't think it's giving up your independence as much as realizing that we all get to a point in our lives where we need someone to help us a little bit. Sometimes it's because of age, sometimes it's because of a financial hardship, sometimes it's because of an illness. You didn't hesitate to get the care needed for Millie when she broke her hip. There's nothing wrong with accepting help. You're ninety-one years old, Dick. That's a lot longer than most people live. And people who do live that long generally end up in a nursing home. I think you'd rather have them come here than have to put you in a home. They just want to make sure you're eating right and being safe."

Dick just nodded his head. Ray had found that was what he did when he no longer wanted to talk about a topic, or he didn't know what else to say. Ray didn't say anything more, he finished his breakfast and went outside to work on the list of things still needing to be done. When Tom got there, he went right to work too. It really wasn't going to take much longer if they both worked their way through the list. Ray wasn't sure if he should just move on and hope that they figured things out between them, or if he should stay. He really wasn't family though, so he didn't have a real reason to be here.

Beth came out to call them in for lunch and explained that she and her father were going to eat and then head to the nursing home. Millie wasn't eating for them, and Dick wanted to go and see if he could encourage her to eat. Beth didn't say it, but Ray could see the concern in her eyes and the fear that this just might be nearing an end.

"Anything that I can do to help, you know I will." Ray said. "I don't want to overstep, but if you think that me pretending to be Daniel is in any way a help or a comfort for Millie, I'd be glad to be there if I'm needed."

"Thank you for that." Beth said. "I don't really know what we'll find but I'll keep in touch and if we think you being there would help, I'll be in touch."

"Whatever is best for all of you." Ray said. "I don't want you to feel like I'm stepping in and pretending to be Daniel if it's going to cause hurt for you, but if you thought it would make things better, then I'm willing to pretend."

"Thanks, I'll let you know." Beth said. They walked inside and ate their lunch. Ray and Tom offered to clean up and do the dishes so that Dick and Beth could get to the nursing home.

"Is it wrong of me to say that I think this is probably the beginning of the end?" Tom asked. "I can't imagine she can last much longer if she won't eat."

"No, I wouldn't imagine so." Ray said. "They could put her on an IV, but I don't know how Beth, or her dad feel about that. If she won't eat, there really isn't much else that can be done."

"I think it's going to be really hard for both of them to let her go, but I also don't think they want to see her hang on for weeks and weeks just being kept alive because of a tube." Tom said.

"It's a tough decision to make." Ray agreed. They took care of the clean-up and the dishes and headed back to working on things around the house. They went up onto the roof to assess the shingle situation and counted how many they thought needed to be replaced, it wasn't a lot and Ray was pretty sure he had seen a pack of them in the garage. It was late enough in the day that they didn't want to start hauling shingles up and getting started on the job, so they decided to start that first thing in the morning.

Tom had talked to Beth and Dick wanted to stay right there with Millie until at least after her supper so Tom invited Ray to go down to the diner for dinner.

"So, are you like a wanderer or what?" Tom asked.

"I guess you could say that" Ray began. "I worked in a corporate job for over twenty years and it was getting old. I kind of felt like I was living my life in a fishbowl, you know."

Tom nodded, "I've never been interested in an office job." Tom stated.

"So, I decided it was time to try something else. I had worked long enough to get my full retirement and I had saved up a decent amount of money over the years. I took some photography classes and sold my house and here I am, taking pictures of national monuments and just the everyday life."

"That's pretty risky, selling your house and all that." Tom said.

"I have a small cabin in the mountains. I kept that in case I ever decided to go back and settle down. But I'm also open to the idea of finding someplace new. I'm not going to make any real commitment until I've seen the whole country and then I'll decide if there's someplace that feels like my new home."

"You don't have any family?" Tom asked.

"Not really. I have a half-brother that I've never met, and I have a cousin that I used to spend time with, but when my dad left, we didn't really have contact with that side of the family anymore and we lost touch." Ray said.

"Are you planning to reconnect?" Tom asked.

"The cousin, definitely, when I get in his area, I'll look him up. The half-brother, I'm not really sure yet." Ray admitted. "How about you, do you have family?"

"Just Beth and our kids and grandkids." Tom said.

By the time they got home, Dick and Beth were there too. Dick had already gone to bed. It was early, but Ray assumed that he was exhausted both from being out most of the day and the emotional strain involved with caring for his wife.

"How is she?" Ray asked.

"She won't eat, or can't eat, whichever way you want to look at it." Beth said. "Dad got her to take a few bites, but it was difficult at best, and she chokes and has a hard time swallowing, or just doesn't even try to swallow. The trigger in her brain doesn't tell her that she needs to swallow sometimes, I guess. That's what the doctor said."

"Are they thinking about putting in an IV?" Tom asked.

"That's kind of up to dad." Beth said. "For now, they are going to keep trying to get at least liquids down her. Dad doesn't want to do an IV if he can help it. She's become so fragile that everything hurts her. It hurts her to have her blood pressure taken. I can't imagine what an IV would do."

"I know sometimes it's harder for the patient to keep them around, but it's harder for the family to let them go." Ray said.

"That's where my dad is right now, I think." Beth said. "He doesn't want to let her go, but he feels like it may be selfish of him to keep her here. For now, she's alert and with it, at least as much as she has been lately. Other than the eating aspect, she's the same woman she's been for the last few weeks. She did ask about Daniel though and wondered if he was ever going to come and visit her."

"So, she still thinks he's alive?" Tom said.

"Apparently, but she also doesn't remember that Ray was there just the other day, or she has realized that he isn't Daniel." Beth said.

"Well, like I said," Ray began, "I'll follow whatever you think is best."

"I think I'm going to spend the night here." Beth said. "You go home and get a good night's rest. I want to be here in case he gets any phone calls."

"Okay," Tom agreed, "Text me a list of what you want me to bring for you in the morning."

"I'm thinking that we may just need to plan to stay here for a while anyway. Maybe this will convince him to let us move in." Beth said. "I don't know, I guess we'll take it day by day."

"Whatever you want babe." Tom said. He gave his wife a kiss on the forehead and headed out the door.

"I'm here if you need to talk, or, I can head to bed if you want to be alone with your thoughts." Ray said.

Beth didn't answer right away, but finally she said, "You know, I always thought my dad would be the first to go. He's had so many health issues over the years. But then mom started showing signs of the dementia. At first it was the little things and then they got bigger and bigger. It took a while for us to realize it was something beyond just the typical forgetfulness that often comes with old age. I mean my dad doesn't remember a lot of things. He's always asking me if I remember the name of someone who went to our church or the person that did this or that. That's typical for his age though I think."

She paused for a long time again, but Ray didn't say anything, she eventually continued on. "With my mom though, it was everyday things. Like I told you the other day. She didn't remember how to cook, or she didn't know what something was called. After she broke her hip, she came home for a while after the rehab, but she had changed so much. And dad didn't want her to fall again. She'd get up in the middle of the night and he'd find her sitting at the kitchen table or wandering down the hall. He was afraid she'd walk out the door someday and possibly get hurt or go missing. That was when he admitted that he couldn't keep her here any longer. It was just too much for him. It about killed him to have to admit that and put her in the nursing home, but he knew it was the safest place for her. He talked about maybe tying to go into a senior apartment or something like that, but they don't really take care of you, they don't provide meals and all that. So, we talked and he decided this was the best plan. He didn't want to have to give up the house and I think somewhere in there he thought maybe she would get better and be able to come back here someday. I think he thought her illness would improve, but he didn't really understand what Alzheimer's is."

"It's definitely something that most people don't understand." Ray agreed. "And its fairly new as far as medical research and working on a cure goes. It's one of those things that I'm sure isn't new, but the understanding of it is."

"Yeah, it's like Autism." Beth said. "One of my grandkids has it, but the label is fairly new. I guess it's good that science and medicine is progressing all the time, but sometimes it almost seems like Alzheimer's is just a new disease that no one had twenty years ago. I know it can't be, or at least I don't see how it can be. But it sometimes seems that way since no one ever heard of it before."

"And with new illnesses, comes new research, but that never seems to move fast enough." Ray said.

"No, it doesn't." Beth agreed. "Well, like I told Tom, I want to be here in case he gets any calls during the night, but I'm exhausted. I'm just going to sleep out here on the couch so I'm close by."

"Okay, if you need me for anything, let me know." Ray said. "I'll be upstairs."

"Thanks Ray." Beth said.

Ray could tell that Beth was both exhausted and sad. This was one of the final stages for Millie. It had to be, if she couldn't or wouldn't eat, she couldn't last much longer. Even an IV could only prolong a life so much. Ray wasn't really sure what to do other than play it by ear. Part of him said that he should move on down the road and let the family do whatever they needed to do. But a part of him knew that Millie firmly believed that he was Daniel at least at times she did and if pretending to be Daniel could bring her even a moment of peace or happiness, then he was happy to stay and visit her in her final days. He would use the days that they didn't feel he needed to be at the nursing home to finish his photographic endeavors and would spend whatever time they needed him to with Millie. He would sit with her if they wanted him to. If it would give her happiness believing that her son was there, then it was well worth it to him to pretend.

The following morning, Dick apologized for not making a breakfast, but he wanted to get to the nursing home and try to help Millie with her breakfast.

"Not so fast, dad." Beth said. "You don't have to make breakfast, but you need to eat some. I won't have you making yourself sick by not eating just because you want to go and try to help mom."

"But it's more important that she eat." Dick argued.

"But delaying it long enough for you to eat isn't going to be an issue." Beth said. "If you get sick and weak, that's not going to help mom. You have to take care of yourself."

"I never wanted to be in this place." Dick said sadly. "I never wanted to have to watch her die."

"I know dad." Beth said putting her arm around him, "I never wanted to have to watch either of you die, but it's a part of life."

"I wanted to go first." Dick said.

"Well, God didn't see it that way." Beth stated. "He knew that mom would need you here to help make her last days as comfortable and as happy as they can be."

Dick just nodded and sat at the table. Within a few minutes, he had a plate of eggs and bacon in front of him. He ate it, but not with any real interest in the food itself. It was more about doing what he had to in order to have Beth let him leave.

As they prepared to go, Dick turned to Ray and asked, "I know I have no right to ask this, but it always makes my Millie happy when you are there. I know that she thinks you're Daniel. But if it's not too uncomfortable for you, would you come and see her today?"

"I'd be glad to do that, Dick." Ray said. "If it makes Millie happy, I don't mind her thinking I'm Daniel. Let me go change really quick." He had dressed for doing yard work, but he would set that aside for however long they wanted him to if his presence made any difference in how Millie faced her final days.

When they walked into Millie's room and Dick approached her bed, she looked at him and said "Where have you been? I haven't seen you in forever. You used to always be here with me, but you haven't come to see me in so long."

"I was here just last night, Millie." Dick said sadly. "I'll always be here for my best girl."

"I don't remember you coming to see me." Millie said. "I don't remember seeing you for a long time."

"I know Millie." Dick said with resolve. "I know you don't remember, but I promise you I won't ever stop coming to see you. I love you more than anything in the world."

"I love you too Dick." Millie said softly. "I don't like it when I have to go so long without seeing you."

Ray could see the change in Dick's demeanor, he knew that the man was feeling like he was already at a loss as to what to do when he didn't have Millie in his life anymore. He knew that Dick knew that Millie not remembering him visiting her just hours ago was just a progression of her dementia. But he could also tell that the man wished he didn't have to cause his wife any pain, perceived or otherwise. Dick would move into this room and stay will Millie until the end if he could. The problem was the end could be days or weeks away. There was no prediction as to how the disease would progress. It was obvious that her mental capacity was diminishing, but if they could get enough nutrition for her, her body could potentially carry on for a while without the memory working. It was all about what triggers were making a connection from brain to body.

Chapter Five

The next few days, Dick, Beth, and Ray spent most of their time with Millie. They weren't always all there, but they alternated. Dick stayed as long as the staff would let him, but they did send him home at night so that he could sleep. She wasn't eating and Dick had refused intervention with an IV. "As much as I hate the thought of losing her," he had told the doctor quietly, "I hate the thought of her being uncomfortable even more. The least little thing causes her pain, I can't imagine what being hooked up to that thing would do. I'll get her to eat and drink as much as I can, but I don't want an IV."

Millie was getting weaker by the day. She still tried to take small bites of soft foods and sips of nutritious drinks, but it seemed like everything was making her choke and then she had to take a break. Ray could see the defeat in Dick's eyes that his wife was obviously past the point of being able to take in enough sustenance to keep her going. She slept most of the time now, but when she did wake, she was always happy to see Dick and the man she thought was her son. For the most part, she was always happy to see Beth too, even though she didn't know who she was. Just having people there made her perk up.

Ray had met all of Beth's children. They had taken their turns to come and see Millie, knowing it was likely to be their last. Only the oldest of Millie's great grand-children had come to see her, the other two were quite young and wouldn't understand anyway.

It took a couple of weeks, but with the small amount of food and liquid she could consume, Millie drifted off into a coma. The doctor had once again offered an IV, if she was unconscious, she wouldn't be aware of the pain anyway. But Dick had chosen to let her go naturally. As much as Ray could tell it pained him to do so, Dick refused to have measures that would prolong her existence. He explained to them that she had stopped living, she was only existing, and he didn't want to make her exist any longer only for his own selfish desire to not have to live without her.

At that point, Dick refused to leave Millie's side other than to go to the bathroom and he used the one in her room. He had his meals by her side. He slept in the recliner next to her bed. He wanted to be there to say his final goodbyes. Beth did the same other than going out to grab food for her and her father. Ray felt odd being there since he wasn't family, but Dick had asked him to come as much as he could, just in case.

Beth spent a lot of time reading, and Ray did too. But Dick spent his time either sleeping or sitting beside Millie holding her hand. One sunny afternoon, Millie opened her eyes and spoke. "Dick?"

He quickly sat up and looked at his wife. "I'm here Millie. What do you need my sweet girl?"

"Dick, it's time for me to go." Millie said.

Dick had tears streaming down his face and he couldn't muster up any words to say. Beth and Ray had moved to Millie's bedside, and she turned their way.

"Beth, oh, Beth." Millie said, her voice was weak, but she added, "You take care of him for me, won't you?"

"I will mom." Beth was crying. "I'll take care of him."

Millie turned to Ray and said, "I need you to be strong. I need you to take care of Daniel's little girl. That girl needs you to take care of things for her, she needs her family."

"I will." Ray said. The woman was obviously in her last moments, it would do no good to not pretend to be her son. He wasn't sure why she was thinking that Daniel had a child because to his knowledge, he hadn't ever had any children, and if he had, the child would be fully grown.

She turned to Dick one last time and said, "Kiss me goodbye Dick, before the angles take me away."

Dick leaned in and kissed her and said, "I love you, Millie."

"I love you too, Dick." Then Millie closed her eyes and her breathing got more and more shallow until it stopped.

Dick sat there for long minutes, holding her hand even though hers had gone limp. Ray made his way down the hall to the nurses' station to let them know that Millie had passed. He asked them if it was okay to let Dick have some more time with her. He wasn't sure what the protocol would be when someone died. He didn't think there would be any reason to rush, but he honestly didn't know.

"He can have time." the nurse Ray had talked to that first day said. "You just let us know when you're ready to leave. But I will say from experience here, it's best if the family encourage him to not sit and dwell on it with the body right there. Part of being able to move past it is being able to walk out of that room. It won't happen in the next few minutes, but the longer he stays there, the harder it is for him to be willing to want to go home. He'd rather just sit there until he can go with her."

Ray understood the man's meaning. Dick could say his goodbyes, but he needed to be taken home and given reasons to go on with his life, or he wouldn't want to go on at all. He needed to be encouraged to remember that he had a daughter and grandkids who wanted him to be in their lives for a while yet.

He walked back into the room and waited for a while, just silently trying to send whatever strength he could to Beth and to Dick. He wasn't sure how long they just sat there, Dick and Beth both crying, but he would stay and support them as much as he could.

Finally, Beth collected herself enough to say, "Dad, we should go home so they can do what they need to do here."

"I don't want to go." Dick snapped.

"I know, Dad, but they need to take care of her now." Beth said. "We'll take you home." She didn't really leave him a lot of room for argument.

"Yeah, Dick, the staff here has things they need to take care of. We'll let them do their jobs and we'll go and start planning for a way to honor her life." Ray added.

Dick reluctantly let go of Millie's hand and leaned down and kissed her on the forehead. He walked out of the room with several long looks back at his wife. His shoulders were slumped, and he had a pronounced shuffle to his walk. He looked more like an old man than he had in the entire time Ray had known him. They finally got him out to the parking lot and into Beth's car. Ray had seen the nurse he had spoken with and given him a nod of thanks for letting Dick have the time to sit with his wife for a while. The man had given a small nod back.

When they got back to the house, Dick had said he wasn't hungry, and he was tired and he made his way into his bedroom and closed the door.

"I'll give him a day at the most, but he's going to eat." Beth said determinedly. "I'm not losing both parents until I have to." She walked out the back door to sit in the yard. Ray was sure both of them needed time to process the events of the day and consider what the future would hold.

He didn't want anyone to feel obligated to feed him dinner, so he went into the diner to grab a meal. A young woman came to his table, and he started to give her his order but she didn't look like she was actually waiting to take it.

"She died, didn't she?" the woman asked.

Ray was puzzled as to why this young woman was asking, but he supposed she had known the family most of her life if she had grown up in this town.

"Yes, she did, she died peacefully a few of hours ago." Ray explained.

The woman looked very sad to hear that.

"Did you know her well?" he asked.

"She was my grandma."

Ray wasn't sure he had heard her right, or maybe she didn't really mean grandma. Maybe it was one of those 'like a grandma to me' type of things. He had met all of Beth's children. "I never knew her before she got sick, but I'm sure she was like a grandma to a lot of people." Ray said.

"Yeah, but she was actually my grandma." the young woman said.

"I'm not sure I understand." Ray said.

"Her son Daniel was my father." she explained. "I never really knew him much, he died when I was little."

You could have knocked Ray over with a feather. He had not expected that at all. "Does your grandpa or your aunt know you?" Ray couldn't imagine that they hadn't wanted her to be a part of the family if they had known. Although if Daniel had been a problem child later in life, it was possible that he either didn't tell them or they hadn't wanted to know.

"No, only my grandma knew. I used to go visit her."

"What's your name?" Ray asked.

"Danielle." she said. "My mom wanted to name me after my dad. He wasn't really a part of my life though."

"But you used to go visit Millie?" he asked.

"Yeah."

"In the nursing home?"

"No, I've been seeing her for years, even before she got sick. I couldn't go see her much in the nursing home." Danielle said.

"So, Millie was the only one that knew you existed?" Ray asked.

"Yeah, she wasn't really sure how my grandpa would take it. I guess my dad and him had a falling out or whatever you want to call it before he died and so my grandma wasn't sure how he'd take it if he knew I was out there. She said he might like having another granddaughter or he might see it as just another screw up that his son did. Having a kid and not taking responsibility for it. She always said I looked just like him though."

"Has he ever seen you in here, or your aunt Beth for that matter?" Ray asked.

"Oh, I don't work here, I know you thought I did when I walked up to your table like that, but I don't. I just saw you walk in, so I followed you. I know you've been going to see her, and I wanted to know." Danielle said.

"Please, have a seat, let me buy you dinner." Ray said.

She hesitated, but finally she sat down. The waitress made her way over and they ordered before they talked anymore.

"So, how old are you?" Ray asked.

"I'm twenty-three." Danielle said.

"You were about three when your dad died?" he asked.

"About that, I don't remember him at all and from what my mom said, he wasn't really interested in being a daddy anyway." she stated.

"I'm sorry to hear that." Ray said. "Is your mom still in the area?"

"No, she died about two years ago." Danielle said. "She had cancer."

"I'm very sorry for your loss." Ray said. "So, your mom told Millie, but no one else in the family?"

"She didn't intentionally tell Millie. From what my mom said, she saw us in the store one day when I was about five and she was sure I had to be Daniel's daughter. She said I looked just like him at that age. And my mom thinks that somewhere along the line, my dad had mentioned me to her. Or maybe he had just told her he had gotten someone pregnant or whatever."

"And you've had a relationship with her for eighteen years?" he asked.

"Kind of" Danielle said. "When I was little, I didn't see her a lot. She stopped by once a month or so and dropped of clothes and things for me, toys, sometimes food. I'd see her at the park watching me sometimes, and I'd say hi. She'd buy me an ice cream or a candy if my mom said it was okay. When I got older and understood who she was, I started asking her if I could see her more. She'd let me stop by her house some days if she knew no one else was going to be there, or we'd meet somewhere for lunch."

"So, you had an ongoing relationship with her?" Ray asked.

"Yeah, when my mom died, she came to the funeral, and she told me that if I ever needed anything to call her. This is a small town, and she didn't want her husband to get upset, so sometimes she'd pick me up and we'd go to the mall in the city and have lunch or whatever. She tried really hard to be a grandma to me within the limits of not wanting everyone to know. I'm not really sure if my grandpa would want to know me, or my aunt. I just know that my grandma said she didn't want to upset the apple cart." Danielle explained. "When she broke her hip and went into the home, they weren't going to let me see her, but she added me to the visitors list. She was still mentally okay at that point. After she started forgetting things, I was still on the list, so I went, but towards the end, my grandpa and my aunt were there more, and I had to be careful. I didn't know what I would have said if they had asked me who I was and why I was there."

Ray was listening to the young woman's story, and the one thing that kept going through his mind was the last thing Millie had said. She had asked him to take care of Daniel's little girl. At first, he had thought she was misspeaking since she had previously thought he was her son and then he thought she was confused about a daughter. But she had been using her last moments to do what she could to help her granddaughter find a place in the family. Millie had been far more lucid in those moments than she had in probably a year. She hadn't called him Daniel; she had asked him to take care of Daniel's daughter. He knew it was her dying wish that somehow her family could be united and not broken like it had been for decades. He wasn't sure how he was supposed to do that, but he knew that Millie had asked him to try.

He got Danielle's contact information and told her about what Millie had asked him in her final moments. "I have to ask if that's what you would want too." Ray began. "I can't guarantee that I can make it happen, but I am willing to try. But it's really up to you if you want to see if this works or not. Obviously, Millie wanted you to be a part of the family, but you have a say in it all too."

"I'd like to at least know them." Danielle began. "I don't know that we'll ever be a close knit family, but I would at least like to know who they are and have them know that I exist."

"Then I'll be in touch." Ray said. "Like I said, no promises, but I can try."

They parted ways and Ray went back to Dick's house. As he expected, Beth was still there with her dad. He was sitting in his recliner looking totally lost and Ray understood that completely.

"I'm sorry I wasn't up to cooking a dinner." Beth said. "I did have some stuff for sandwiches if you need anything."

"No, I went to the diner, I didn't want anyone to feel like they needed to take care of me at a time like this." Ray said. He figured everyone was too tired and too emotional to bring up Danielle tonight. He'd wait a day or two before he said anything. She had promised that she would wait to hear from him before she did anything or made any effort to approach them herself. She was hoping to not be a problem at the funeral though, because she did want to go to that. "I'm just going to head upstairs if that's okay. I don't want to intrude. I've got some emails and things to deal with anyway. I have to see what my friend thinks of the photos and if there's anything more that he wants taken."

"Sure, thanks for being there today, Ray." Beth said.

"It was no problem at all." Ray stated. "I'll see you in the morning. I assume you have arrangements to make."

"We do." Beth said sadly. "We definitely do."

Ray went upstairs and decided it wasn't late, so he would try doing a video chat with Maude. She had been a good sounding board when he had been in Thousand Palms. He wasn't sure if she would be near her device.

He had gotten it for her so she could keep in touch with her kids and her grandkids. He wasn't sure if she had it around much when it wasn't time for a call with one of them. He sent the request through anyway.

"Hello, Ray." Maude said. "It's good to see you."

"It's good to see you too Maude." Ray said. "How are things there?"

"They're pretty good." she replied. "Hope's been doing really well. She's getting so healthy. She's putting on weight and in her case, that's a good thing. It wouldn't be good for most of us, but it is for her. She had gotten too thin for it to be healthy."

"I know, Maude." Ray agreed. "I'm glad to hear she's doing well. I have a situation I'd like to get your thoughts on if I can."

"Oh sure, I'd be happy to help in any way if you think I'm able." Maude said.

Ray explained the current situation to Maude and asked, "I want to tell them, I think they have a right to know. I don't know if right now is the time though. Millie just died. Is it good timing to tell them now?"

"Well, in some ways, there's never going to be a good time, but on the other hand, now is the best time. They're all grieving, let them have the opportunity to grieve together." Maude said. "I know that if she was my blood, I'd want to know. The situation with the son going bad be damned, that girl is part of their family. They have the right to know, and they have the right to grieve their lost together."

"Thanks, Maude. I knew I could count on you to tell it to me straight." Ray said.

"I always do, some people think I'm harsh, but I've just never seen any reason to beat around a bush when you can just move straight ahead."

They spent a few more minutes catching up on what Ray was taking pictures of and where he thought he would go next before he wished Maude a good night and thanked her again for her advice. He knew he had to tell Dick and Beth; he just wasn't sure how to go about it. He'd sleep on it and maybe an opportunity would present itself in the morning.

Chapter Six

Ray went downstairs not really sure what to expect. He didn't know if anyone would be up and if they were up would they still be home or would they have gone to the funeral home to start on the funeral arrangements. He found Beth in the kitchen, but Dick was nowhere to be seen.

"Where's your dad?" he asked.

"He's sleeping finally. He sat in that chair most of the night, but I finally talked him into taking some Tylenol PM and going to lay down. I told him he needs to try to look a little less exhausted when we meet the funeral director." Beth said. "Did you need something?"

"I've been doing a lot of thinking." Ray began. "The last thing that Millie said to me was about taking care of Daniel's daughter. What if he does have a daughter?"

"Well, I assume it was all part of her dementia." Beth said. "She said a lot of things over the last several months that made no sense."

"But think about it," Ray encouraged. "She didn't call me Daniel like she has been. She knew I wasn't her son, but she did ask me to take care of his daughter. If she had implied that I was Daniel or that she was referring to my daughter, I would agree with you that it was part of the Alzheimer's or whatever that made her not remember that Daniel was dead, and she was just having delusional thoughts. But the fact that she knew I wasn't him, makes me think that she may have been more lucid in those last moments than she had been for a long time."

"I get what you're saying, but why would she think Daniel had a child?" Beth asked.

"Because he did, or at least I believe that he did, and your mom knew her." Ray said.

Beth sat down with a puzzled look on her face. "What makes you think so?"

"Well, I've met her." Ray began, "at least I believe I have. She told me her story last night at the diner and I think what she says is true. And I've only seen a few photos of your bother, but in my opinion, she looks a lot like him."

"What's this person's name?" Beth asked.

"Her name is Danielle. She said her mom wanted to name her after her father." Ray stated.

"I've heard that name." Beth said. "When my mom first started forgetting things, she'd sometimes ask about Danielle. We just assumed it was someone from her childhood or early years because none of us had ever heard the name. There were times when she was sure she was still in high school or just newly married. The name wasn't anyone we knew, so we just kind of went along with it and said, 'oh she's fine' or 'she's doing well, I saw her in town'. We never thought Danielle was a real person."

"She's very real and if her story is true, she's your niece." Ray said. "She told me stories of Millie taking her to the mall and Millie dropping of clothes for her when she was little since Daniel died when the child was quite young. Although she also said that he didn't really pay much attention to her when he was alive."

"That part I would believe." Beth said. "My brother had taken a pretty deep fall from being the perfect son long before he died. He would get involved in one thing or another and end up broke or needing a lawyer. He never did anything big; it was always smaller stuff like minor drug possession or things like that. I wouldn't put it past him to have had a child and not take responsibility for it."

"She doesn't want anything from any of you other than the right to be at her grandmother's funeral. But I will say her mother died from cancer a couple of years ago and I didn't get the impression that she had much family in her life. I think she'd love to be a part of this one, but she doesn't expect it to happen." Ray said.

"I'd like to meet her before we mention it to my dad." Beth said. "He doesn't need anymore upset right now if she isn't the real deal. Do you have a way to contact her?"

"I do." Ray said. "She gave me her number and I told her I'd keep in touch."

"We're supposed to meet with the funeral director tomorrow." Beth said. "Can you see if she can meet us after dinner tonight. I can get Tom or one of the kids to come stay with my dad. I don't know, I'll say I need to run home for a few things or something."

"I can do that." Ray said.

"You'll go with me won't you, since you've talked to her already."

"Of course, I'd be glad to." Ray agreed.

"Set it up for eight." Beth said.

"Will do."

At just after eight that evening, Ray and Beth were seated at a table in the small town diner. Beth was facing the door. When Danielle walked in, Beth's face turned white as a sheet. "That's her."

That was all she said, but Ray looked up and smiled as Danielle made her way to their table. He stood to greet her. "Hello, Danielle." he gestured for her to take a chair. "Please, have a seat. Would you like anything?"

"Just water thanks." she said.

Beth still hadn't really said anything, she was just kind of staring with her mouth open.

"Beth, this is Danielle. Danielle, this is Beth." Ray said, hoping that hearing her name would break Beth's shock at seeing her niece.

"It's nice to meet you." Danielle said.

"You too, sorry, I just can't believe that you look exactly like my brother." Beth said. "It's like you're a female version of him."

"My mom said I looked just like him. Grandma did too. I don't remember him really. I think I have vague pictures in my mind of what he looked like, but I don't know if that's from pictures grandma showed me or if I actually remember him from when I was really little." Danielle said.

"How old are you?" Beth asked.

"I'm twenty-three."

"So, you were just a toddler when he died." Beth said. "When did you start spending time with my mom?"

"Honestly, I don't remember that either. She was just kind of this nice lady that showed up and brought me clothes or toys when I was little." Danielle said. "I remember when I was about to start school in kindergarten, she took my mom and me to the city and bought my school clothes. I was always trained to thank someone for nice things, so I thanked her, and she told me that she was happy to do it, that was what grandmas did. At the time, I don't think I understood that she actually was my grandma, I just thought she was a grandma and was being nice to me because my mom never had a lot of extra money. We ate and always had a roof over our heads, but the things like school clothes and all that would have been harder for her to do."

"So, you've known her most of your life. Did she say why she never told us about you?" Beth asked.

"She said that she didn't think that my grandfather would understand. According to her, he had some sort of falling out with my dad and she didn't think he would welcome me into the family because of his feelings about my dad." Danielle said. "She never really mentioned anything about wanting me to meet you or not wanting me to meet you. It was more about not wanting your dad to know and that probably meant not telling you because the more people that know a secret, the harder it is to keep."

"That makes sense, but it's the first I'm hearing about a falling out." Beth said. "I do know that my brother made a lot of really poor choices in the last half of his life. And I know neither of my parents were happy with those choices, but my mom was by far the one that could overlook things and love anyway. I don't mean that my dad didn't love him, but he was the harder nut to crack as they say. He knew that his son had been raised to do better, and he chose not to. I've always wondered if in some ways that made him feel like a failure. It shouldn't because it's not his fault what either of us decided to do as adults, but as a parent, I get that sometimes you question whether or not you did things the right way."

"I guess I never really blamed anyone for things. My life was good. My mom loved me enough for both of them I think." Danielle said. "I guess I knew that I had a dad, but I knew that he died when I was little. I didn't really dwell on it; it just was what it was."

"Do you have any siblings?" Beth asked.

"Nope, it's just me."

Beth was quiet for several minutes and Ray could tell that she was still trying to process everything. Finally, she said, "I want to tell my dad, but I don't really know how, and I'm not sure that right now is the right time to do it."

"That's fine," Danielle said. "I don't want to intrude on the family's time. I would like to be at the funeral if that's okay."

"That's definitely okay." Beth said. "She was your grandmother and she obviously cared about you. She would want you there. I just may not say anything to my dad until after. I have to play that part by ear."

"I understand." Danielle agreed. "As much as I would love to have a relationship with him, I can accept it if he doesn't feel the same way. Or if you think it's too much for him to handle at his age. I can respect that."

"I honestly have to say that I have to play it by ear right now." Beth said. "I don't think he's ready for me to go home and tell him right now, but I also can't say that it won't feel right tomorrow. I will tell my husband and children. I want them to know their cousin. I was adopted and I always felt like family needed to know family."

"I'd love to meet them." Danielle said.

"We'll arrange it sometime soon then." Beth said, "Although most likely not until after the funeral, we all have to get past that first. Speaking of that, I hate to run, but I have to get home and get some rest. Tomorrow, I have to take dad down to the funeral home to start the arrangements. Danielle, it was great to meet you. I just wish I had known about you, years ago."

"Please let me know when the funeral will be." Danielle said as they all stood to leave.

Ray dropped money on the table to pay for the coffee they had. That was one thing that he loved about the small towns he had visited. You could leave the money without the fear of the bill never getting paid because someone else picked it up. You couldn't always count on that in the big city. Most people wouldn't take the money, but you could never be completely positive in a bigger city.

They walked out and Beth and Danielle did a sort of awkward one arm hug. But Ray was happy to see that they were both trying to make their way through a really difficult situation. A man who had died twenty years ago had left a mess in the wake of his poor choices and now these two women had to try to figure out a way forward. He was sure that if they both wanted it to work, and it seemed like they did, that they would find their way. It wouldn't be easy, but he was sure it could happen.

Chapter Seven

Ray and Tom worked on the things around the house while Beth and Dick went to make the arrangements. Apparently, Dick and Millie had gone to a church for years although they hadn't attended as much in the last few years. The church wanted to take care of a meal after the funeral.

That night, after dinner, Tom and Beth went home to take care of some things around their own home, and Ray sat with Dick in the living room. He didn't want the man to feel all alone, so he would stay however long he was needed.

"You know, my Millie, she was a sharp one." Dick began. "Money, she knew how to handle money like no one I've ever seen. If she had done anything during the day, she sat down at night with her receipts and her purse and go though and make sure every nickel was accounted for. We used to tease her because she would sit and say, 'now where did I spend a dollar and twenty-seven cents.' But she wouldn't rest until she figured it out. She had paper after paper of what money was going to come in and what money needed to go out and what she was saving money for this or that. It all looked like hen scratch to me, but Millie knew every jot and tittle of where things were."

"She sounds like a smart woman." Ray stated.

"And I never could understand, I didn't make good money, but somehow she always figured things out. She made sure we had a good vacation every year when the kids were growing up. We went to Florida and took them to Disney and all of that. I know I didn't make enough money for that to have been easy. She'd put pennies in a jar and turn them in when the jar got full. She'd set that aside because no one misses a penny, but those pennies sure added up. She'd take in things that could be recycled for the deposit or whatever they were paying for it, and it never went back into the budget, it went into the vacation account. I remember there was an amusement park not far from here and for a couple of years, they had a promotion that if you brought in a certain kind of pop can, they'd give you something off of your ticket. I don't remember if it was five dollars or ten. I was always working when Millie took them on day trips like that. But Millie would buy that kind of pop, and every single one of them drank their can so that they could get a ticket. She did that with the grandkids too."

Ray was getting a clearer picture of just who Millie was and how she had tried to make it up to Danielle that she didn't get to go to the places and have the opportunities the others had had. "I'm sure she was a wonderful grandma."

"Oh, she was. She was such a good mother. She was raised in a home where there wasn't a lot of frivolity. Of course, she was born right after the great depression and times were tough. I think she got a lot of her frugality from her momma. None of their family was overly showy with their emotions, I think they were just raised to be serious and focus on school and the things that mattered. Her momma was a teacher in a one room schoolhouse when she was young. She'd been married to a man who was abusive, and she divorced him. That wasn't heard of in those days. But she did, and she went to school to become a teacher. She graduated from the first class of teachers at the State University. She was a determined woman and she taught that to her children. She married a good man the second time, he was a hard worker. But they were a very disciplined family. That's not to say that they didn't have any fun, they did. But they knew the value of a dollar and they knew the value of working for that dollar."

Dick sat silent for a few minutes, thinking about memories of his wife. "I used to see her walking to school, I stopped going to school after the sixth grade. I didn't like school and there was always work to be done on the farm, so my mom didn't make me go back. She was happy to have the extra help at home. I'm one of the youngest ones, so most of my siblings were getting married and moving out on their own by that time. We raised chickens and cows, sometimes pigs. We always had a garden for fresh vegetables, and she canned enough to last throughout the winter. But I'd be driving into town for one reason or another, and I'd see Millie and her sister walking to school, and I just thought she was about the prettiest thing that ever walked the earth. She was only fourteen when I started asking her to go to dances and things with me. Her momma wouldn't let us go out alone for a long time. In fact, when she first asked her mother to let her go out with me, her momma thought she was talking about one of my older brothers and told her she couldn't go out with a married man. She had to explain just who I was."

"But she finally got it sorted out." Ray said.

"She did, and I'll tell you, everyone loved Millie. Even my own brothers went and told her that if I ever did anything bad to her to tell them and they would teach me a lesson. I was kind of a rough guy back then I guess. I think I always felt like I had to be tough. I was shorter, I was younger, I had to find a way to hold my own, I guess. But I would have never hurt Millie. I think probably my brothers knew that, but they were always watching out for me and wanted to make sure I didn't do anything stupid."

Again, Dick sat quietly lost in his memories for a while, but Ray didn't make any effort to push him to talk. He just waited patiently for the man to talk or not talk, whichever he needed to do.

"My Millie really was good with money and keeping books, she never took a class in it, it just came natural to her. She worked for a few small businesses in town and even kept the books for the church we attended for years. Everyone knew that Millie was as honest as the day was long, and she could spot an error with the accuracy of a bloodhound. Everyone else would be sitting there scratching their heads, and Millie would look at it for five minutes and show them exactly where someone had made the mistake. I remember one Sunday; we brought the offering money home so that Millie could take it and deposit it in the bank the next day and someone broke into our house and took that money. Millie felt so bad about that that she never did bring the money home again, or if she did, she hid it really well. We figured it had to be someone who knew us because nothing else had been taken. Just that bag of cash and checks. But Millie felt responsible for it just the same. We filed a police report, and they came and looked around, the church had insurance so it ended up getting taken care of, but Millie felt personally responsible for that for a long time. Everyone tried to tell her that it wasn't her doing, but she somehow felt it was."

"Well, she was a good woman with a conscience, she felt responsible for things put in her care." Ray agreed. "I hope she didn't give up taking care of the books and things, it sounds like she was really good at it."

"No, the pastor convinced her to not give it up," Dick said. "He told her that they knew it wasn't her fault. Back in those days, people just didn't lock things up like they do now. Everyone locks everything up and has safes and alarm systems, but that wasn't how it was back then. You trusted your neighbors and you didn't think strangers would just walk into a house and do that. We knew it happened in the city, but we had never had anything taken, not a dime, until that happened. That's why the police said it was probably someone who knew that Millie did that for the church and had come looking specifically for that money bag. They opened cupboards and drawers until the found what they were looking for and then put everything back neat as a pin. We had no idea anything had happened until Millie went to get the money to take it to the bank. She left it in the locked church from then on and made the extra time to go pick it up there to take it to the bank."

"Didn't they have a night drop box?" Ray asked.

"Oh, I think they did, but there was always a lot of cash money in there and Millie didn't want to take a chance on the deposit being wrong. She would take it to the bank and stand and watch the teller count it to make sure they came up with the same amount she had before she would take the deposit receipt. If they were off by even a dime, she would ask them to recount it. She didn't want the church to be shorted."

Again, there was a pause as Dick traveled through the memories in his mind. "I didn't know half of what she was doing with the money because I didn't understand most of it. I knew that we always had what we needed and some of what we wanted. The lights were always on and the house was always warm, there was a hot dinner waiting for me every night. That was all that I knew. When Millie started having trouble with her memory, I found out things that I hadn't ever really paid attention to. She had accounts at a few different banks. Looking back, I can remember her saying that she was going to open an account at this bank because they had better rates on a car loan we were thinking about taking out or she was going to put money in this credit union because then she could get a discount at the eye doctor or some such thing. I just never really understood the depth of what all she had done. When I started checking the mail, it was overwhelming to me. I had to have Beth sit down and sort it all out with me."

"She sounds like a shrewd money manager." Ray offered.

"Oh, she was so smart with money and other things too." Dick said. "When she started losing her memory, I wished I had paid more attention to it all so that I could have helped her. She sometimes would see me with some money and say things about how she always was the one that did that. If I had understood it more, I would have tried to let her feel like she was still doing it, but I would have made sure it was right. I just didn't ever want to pay attention and so when it came down to her not knowing how anymore I had to turn it over to Beth. I always have some cash, but Beth takes care of the banking and paying the bills."

Ray really didn't know what to say. He was sure that Millie hadn't really understood that she had lost the ability to take care of the finances anymore but seeing a dollar bill or whatever denomination it was had stirred some sort of connection or memory in her brain. He just sat and listened to whatever Dick wanted to tell him, the old man needed the time to process his wife's death. Ray didn't care if he sat there and told the same story over and over again, if it was what kept the man from wallowing in sorrow, Ray would gladly listen.

Several more minutes went by before he said, "She was a good cook too. Oh, not anything fancy, but there was always a hot meal on the table when I got home at night. I was a simple meat and potatoes man and she always made sure that dinner was ready within five minutes of when I pulled in from work. I'd walk in and I'd give her a kiss and she'd tell me dinner was almost ready. Even when she was doing those bookkeeping jobs, she made sure that they knew that she could only work certain hours. She worked when the kids were at school and in the summer, she took Beth with her most of the time, Daniel was already pretty much doing his own thing by then. It was only a few hours here and there, but she always made sure the children were cared for. I remember when we first brought Beth home, Millie didn't want to miss church, but she was nervous about taking such a small one. She knew everyone was going to want to hold the baby. They always do. I don't know if it was because we had lost some of our own babies that she was so protective of Beth or if it was just something new. When Daniel was born, we didn't go to church. We hadn't gotten saved yet, so it was only family that we were around when he was a baby. Daniel didn't want us to take his little sister anywhere either, he didn't want to share her. The kids were eight years apart, but they were close when they were little. But then Daniel got old enough to date and was a teenager and he didn't want his little sister around so much. They grew apart, I suppose most do with that much of an age gap between them."

Dick was quiet for a long while and Ray wondered if he had drifted off to sleep. But finally, he spoke again. "I don't know if I did the right thing putting Millie in a home like that and me not going with her. Beth offered to move in to help out, but I didn't want to be an inconvenience to her. I still don't, but I'm not sure I can stay alone anymore. I don't want to go into a home and die there like Millie did."

"I'm sure Beth wouldn't consider it an inconvenience, Dick." Ray assured. "She wouldn't have offered if she didn't want to do it. As to whether or not you did the right thing with Millie, I think you did what you thought was best and no one ever knows for sure what the what if's will be. Millie may have lived longer if she had been here, then again, without the nursing staff around, she might have had another fall or gotten sick here at home.

I'm sure she knew that you did what you thought was best."

"When we used to date, her sister and a friend had to go with us as chaperones, I guess. Millie's mom always said that I could take her, but the sister needed a ride too." Dick began. "I was just interested in doing whatever I had to to be able to take Millie to the dance or whatever that I didn't care who else needed to ride along. I remember one night, we were all coming home from a dance, and I got a flat tire. I was a poor man back then and was usually driving some sort of junker that I had tinkered with enough to get it to run. I didn't have a jack in the car, so I found this old fence post alongside the road, and I got a cinder block out of my trunk. I had Millie stay in the car, I didn't want her pretty dress getting ruined. I put that post on the cinder block and put it under the car. I made her sister and the friend sit at the end of that post to be counterweight and keep the car off the ground. I thought for sure her momma would skin me alive for that one because we got home way past her curfew. When she and her sister told the story, their momma said that she believed them because that story was too crazy for anyone to have just made up on their own. I've done a lot of crazy things in my lifetime. I shouldn't have come out alive of some of them, but for some reason, the good Lord saw fit to not only keep me alive, but to give me sixty-eight years of marriage to Millie. I didn't deserve her, I know I didn't, but I was a blessed man to have won her heart."

Again, Dick sat for a long time, but finally, he said, "I'm going to go to bed, Ray. I'd be honored if you'd be willing to be one of Millie's pallbearers. It means more to me than you can ever know that you let Millie live out her last days being able to spend time with her son. You never once let on that you weren't Daniel, and I think that gave her a peace that she hasn't had in a long time. Even though Daniel was a problem child for a long time before he died, she was able to die believing that he had redeemed himself and that he cared deeply for his mother."

"I'd be happy to do that, Dick." Ray said. "I enjoyed spending time with Millie and letting her believe she had more time with her son. And thank you for the stories you told me tonight, I feel like I've gotten a chance to know her even more through your obvious love for her. If you need anyone to talk to in the night, you just call out for me."

"I appreciate that, Ray." Dick said. "I'll see you in the morning."

"Good night."

Chapter Eight

Millie's funeral wasn't hugely attended, but then again, at her age, most of her peers were already gone or were in nursing homes or not able to get out much. Her church was fairly well represented by the minister and a few of the other leaders. Because there weren't a lot of people, Danielle kind of stood out although she didn't try to in any way. She was the only person under forty in the room other than Beth's adult children and their children.

She came in quietly, made her way to the casket and stood quietly for a minute before taking her seat to wait for the service to begin. Beth hadn't wanted to draw any special attention to the young woman, so she had just given her a small smile and a head nod. Ray had tried to be inconspicuous and did the same. Just before the service started, Dick leaned over to Ray and said, "That young woman who came in a few minutes ago, would you please go ask her to sit with the family."

Ray was kind of puzzled, but he said, "Of course." He walked the few rows back and asked Danielle to come with him.

Danielle thought that maybe they were going to ask her to leave, but instead, Ray escorted her to the front row. She started to sit on the other side of Ray, but Dick motioned for her to sit next to him. Ray took the seat on her other side.

Dick leaned over and said, "You're Daniel's daughter, aren't you?"

"Yes, I am." Danielle admitted. She was stunned at his question, but she wasn't going to lie to him.

"I always thought I would meet you some day. I wasn't sure if you were even in this area anymore, but I had hoped to meet you." Dick said. "Millie always thought that she was hiding things from me, and I understand why. Your father and I didn't part ways in the best of circumstances. But I don't hold that against you. Millie never did tell me, until she started to lose her memory and then she would say things, but I was never really sure whether you were real or not. When you were little, I'd ask about the things she bought and she would say that they were for a little girl that she saw at the park sometimes who didn't seem to have much. I would have never begrudged her helping out anyone who was less fortunate. She never told me that you were our grandchild, until she was starting to confuse things and then I wasn't sure if she was right or if things were muddled. When you walked in that door, I knew that she had to have been talking about you. I have my guesses as to why Millie never said anything, but I do want to have a chance to know you now."

"I'd like that." Danielle said.

Ray leaned back and looked in Beth's direction behind the two. Beth was looking at him with a look that was probably just as confused as his own. They had thought that they were going to have to try to figure out how to break the news to Dick, but he had somehow kind of known all along.

The funeral was a simple thing and then they all went to a short graveside service. Ray offered for Danielle to drive his car over. As a pallbearer, he would be riding in one of the cars provided by the funeral home. He told her she would be doing him a favor since it would allow him to have his own vehicle to get back with. He wasn't sure she would be ready to be in the same car with her newly found family. Not that she had known him much longer, but he didn't have a horse in the race as they say. She didn't have any reason to make a good impression on him. She might feel pressured to try to fit in with them. She accepted his offer with thanks.

At the cemetery, he noticed that while Danielle was seated with the family, she looked stiff and unsure of her place among them. That was completely to be expected though. Just because Dick had seemed to want to form a relationship with her, she was technically still an outsider at this point. Ray had assumed that her appearance had been what had told Dick who she was, but just because she had their blood, it didn't mean that Dick was fully ready to embrace the idea of Daniel's daughter being a part of his life. Ray would do his best to support Danielle in whatever happened. He hoped it was a good outcome for all of them.

After getting the casket into its place, Ray moved in behind the family to stand. There were only a few chairs, and he didn't want to take one of them from someone who might need it more than he did.

The service was brief, and then the officiant invited everyone to the church fellowship hall for a luncheon. Danielle had given Ray his keys back, but she had asked to ride back with him so she could get her car. This had kind of been Ray's plan all along. It gave him time to talk to her without the others around.

"Danielle, I just want you to know that I'm here if you need to talk or if you need a buffer between you and the rest of your family. I'm sure it's been sort of like a whirlwind, and with Millie's death, everyone's emotions are running in all different directions. Just before she died, your grandma asked me to take care of you and that's what I am hoping to do. At the time we were all confused, or I guess it would be more accurate to say that we thought she was, but now that I've met you, I feel like I need to honor that request. I know that you don't know me at all, but I promise you can talk to me about anything or if I can help in any way, please let me know what you need." Ray said as they drove. "I didn't know anyone in this family a month ago. I don't have a vested interest in the outcome other than to hope that it is a good and happy one. I won't take their side if there is a disagreement, in fact, I'm more likely to take yours because I feel like you don't have anyone out there who is on your side. Not that anyone is taking sides, but I'm sure there will be lots of questions and things might get uncomfortable at times." Ray felt like he wasn't really saying what he was hoping to say, but he hoped that the young woman understood where he was coming from. The conversation was done for now though, Ray had driven Danielle to the funeral home to pick up her car so that she could leave the luncheon whenever she felt she was ready to go.

The luncheon was attended by the same people that the funeral had been. There were people who were stocking the food for the small line of people and what Ray assumed to be other church members there for clean up or other duties to make the luncheon run smoothly.

Danielle had walked into the fellowship hall much the same way she had walked into the funeral home. Ray could see the look of determination on her face that she knew she had every right to be there, and no one would easily dissuade her from that, but she also didn't have an air that said she was comfortable with what her role was since it hadn't really been determined yet. She got into the end of the serving line for the food. The family had been told to go first, but she hadn't taken it upon herself to assume that included her. She wasn't really sure who Dick and Beth would want to know who she truly was. She didn't want to jump into the 'family' line and have everyone get curious as to why she was there.

As she left the line with her plate, she seemed happy to see that Ray was at a table with a few empty chairs. Dick and Beth were at a table that was full. Beth's husband and some of her children and grandchildren had every seat taken. It gave Danielle the perfect place to sit and the perfect way to sidestep any questions that may arise if she was with the family all the time. People might start to ask who she was and until they had a chance to sit down and figure out the logistics for themselves, she didn't want any of them to be put in a position of having to try to explain it to someone else.

"Is this seat taken?" she asked as she neared Ray.

"I was saving it for you." Ray said with a smile.

When she was seated and started arranging her silverware and things, Ray said, "You know, I've asked you a lot about your connection to Millie, but I haven't really gotten to know anything about you. Do you work? What types of things keep you busy?"

"I work at the library in town." Danielle said. "I was always a huge reader, so it seemed like the perfect fit. I worked there some during the summer and stuff when I was growing up, but it became full time after I graduated. I'm also doing some online classes. We don't really have options for going to school close by and I didn't want to move. I guess I wanted to be here for Millie. I'm not sure if I'll change my situation or not."

"I'd hold off on that, unless you really want to go away to go to school. If you do then that's great, but don't let Millie being gone be part of that decision. You still have family here and although it may take time for everyone to find their spot in the new situation, I believe it's worth waiting it out to see. Everyone is going to be dealing with both the loss of Millie and the addition of you. Just be patient, but above all, Danielle, be true to yourself. I learned a long time ago that it does no one any good if you try to be what you think they want you to be. If you find something that doesn't feel right, take care of yourself first. Take it in baby steps if you need to, but so far, I don't see anything that tells me they are going to reject you. I think today is not the day to try to form any long term attachments, but I also saw the way Dick looked at you when I was sure he knew who you were. He's had suspicions that you were out there and now that he knows, I believe he wants to get to know you. It may take him a few days to reach out or to try to make progress, but that's understandable in this situation." Ray said. "I think I'm rambling and I'm not sure I'm making much sense, but I guess all of that was to try to say, don't be in a hurry either way. Don't assume it's going to happen tomorrow, but also don't assume it's doomed to fail if it doesn't."

"I get it, I'm not in any hurry." Danielle said. "I wouldn't be going away to school until next year anyway if I did go. I'm doing great with the online classes for now. I can keep doing that until I know for sure what I want to do."

"Good." Ray said. "I'm not exactly sure how much longer I'm going to be in town. I'm going to make another day trip up to the canyon for a few more photos. I'm thinking I may even do an overnight so that I can get the sunrise and sunset, but I'm not sure about that yet. I may do that on my way to my next destination."

"What is your next destination?" Danielle asked.

"I'm not completely sure." Ray stated. "I just kind of hit the road and go where it takes me. I have a list of monuments and things that I hope to see and things I have been asked to take photos of, but I don't have a set path to travel."

"That sounds like fun." Danielle said. "I've always just lived here in this small town. Other than going into the city to shop, I haven't really done much."

"Well, I put in my time in corporate America, I worked in an office in the same building in the same city for my entire adult life until just a couple of months ago. But if there's one thing I've learned, it's that if you set a goal and work towards it you can achieve anything you want to do. You have to put in the work, but it can happen." Ray encouraged.

"Are you saying that you think I will find a place in this family?" Danielle asked.

"I think if that's what you want and that's what you work towards, it will happen. It may not happen tomorrow. It's all very new to them. You've known about them your whole life, but they just found out about you. Beth has known for a few days; Dick has known for a few hours. But he obviously has some desire to know you. He asked you to sit with them." Ray stated.

Danielle was quiet but Ray didn't push for anything more. She was eating and he was sure she had a lot on her mind. For years, she had known these people existed, but she had no real clue as to who they were other than any stories her grandmother may have told her. And a time of loss was never a good time to try to sort through any other emotions.

Several minutes later, Beth walked over to their table she addressed Ray first, "We're going to take my dad home. It's been a long day. Don't feel like you have to rush home though. I'm sure he'll be asleep in no time." She turned to Danielle and said, "My dad, well, all of us would like the opportunity to get to know you. Maybe in a few days after we've all had time to rest and process I can give you a call and set something up?"

"That would be great." Danielle said.

"I'll get your number from Ray, and I'll be in touch." Beth said before walking away.

Ray felt like things would move in a positive direction and he didn't really plan to intervene other than to try to be there for Danielle if she needed to talk to anyone. He hadn't really had any family for a long time, and he knew that she may very well need someone to talk to at times.

Chapter Nine

Ray had decided that one of the best things he could do for the family was to give them time to heal in whatever way they needed to. Having him hanging around might make them feel obligated to cook a meal or to spend time visiting with him. The work on the house was done for the most part, there were just a few items that weren't really pressing to get done and he had no doubt that Tom could handle them all. He figured this was a good time to give them a couple of days without having to worry about anything but processing their grief and their finding their own way forward.

When they were at the breakfast table that morning, he said, "I'm going to head further up the canyon for a couple of days. I want to get photos of both sunset and sunrise if I can. I'll stay in a hotel somewhere up there, but if you need me, I'm just a phone call away." He wanted to make it sound like work really was calling him, and not make them feel like he thought he was in their way.

"Okay." Beth said. "I need to get that phone number from you before you go." She didn't say anything more, and Ray didn't push it. They both knew that she wanted the number for Danielle, but she wouldn't use it until Dick was ready to start the process of getting to know his granddaughter.

Ray packed a small duffel bag with enough clothing for a few days and then headed out to the canyon. He would find a hotel and stay for at least one night. He would decide after he drove around and got some photos if he wanted to stay there longer or if he wanted to try for a different position.

As he was driving toward the small overlook that he had seen on his map, his phone rang. He pulled into the parking lot of a convenience store so that he could give the phone his full attention. "Hello"

"Hi Ray!" the boy said excitedly, "It's Lance. I wanted to call and see how you're doing."

"I'm great, Lance." Ray said. "How are you? How's your mom?"

"We're doing really good." Lance said.

"How's Lucky?"

"He's great. He's learning so much. He can sit and roll over and a whole bunch of stuff." Lance exclaimed. "He's the best dog ever."

"I'm glad to hear that." Ray said.

"Where are you now?" Lance asked. "I really miss hanging out with you."

"I know, I miss it too, but I need to take pictures for my work." Ray didn't explain that it wasn't really work, it was more of a hobby. He didn't have to send photos in, but he was enjoying doing it and he was getting paid for anything that got used in magazines or travel information. Lance was just more likely to understand it better if Ray made it sound like work. "I'm taking pictures of the Grand Canyon today. It's huge. I never imagined it was this big. You know, you've read about it in school, but it's a lot bigger than I realized it was. I'll send some pictures to your mom's email so you can see it. I may not be able to send them for a couple of days, but I'll be sure and send them."

"Okay, cool." Lance said.

Ray could tell that the boy didn't really have a specific topic to talk about, he just wanted to talk. "How's school going? You been playing basketball with your friends?"

"School's okay." Lance said. "We play basketball sometimes on Saturday. I'm supposed to meet the guys at the park in a while."

"That sounds like a good plan for a Saturday." Ray said. "How's your aunt and uncle?"

"There doing good." Lance said. "They keep talking about maybe getting a kid. I hope they get one close to my age so I have someone to hang out with."

"Well, if they get someone younger, you can be the older cousin and show them the ropes." Ray offered. He knew that Sally was hoping to take in a foster child and maybe even adopt. They weren't necessarily looking for a baby, but he didn't think they were looking for a teen or preteen either.

"Yeah." Lance agreed. "I can help the kid out."

"That will be nice of you Lance, I'm sure they will appreciate it."

"Well, I guess I should let you get back to work, I just wanted to let you know that I miss you." Lance said.

"I miss you too Lance, you call me anytime as long as your mom says it's okay." Ray said.

"Okay, bye Ray. I hope you come and visit us again sometime."

"I'm sure I will, Lance. But if you need anything you let me know." Ray stated. He wasn't going to say it, but he hoped Lance would call him if Hope ever got messed up with drugs again. They hung up the call and Ray decided he might as well go into the convenience store and get some cold beverages to put in his cooler. It could get really hot around the canyon.

He got into the checkout line with several bottles of water and tea and a bag of ice in the small basket he had grabbed when he had walked in. He heard a little girl asking her mom if she could have one of the ice cream bars in the freezer right next to the cash register.

"Can I please have the chocolate one mommy?" she begged.

"Not today honey." the woman said. Ray watched as she counted out a whole stack of change that she had placed on the counter.

The young kid behind the register rolled his eyes as she continued to count. "Look, ma'am, we have other customers, can you hurry up." He said with impatience.

"Oh, I'm in no hurry." Ray said. "You take your time." He wanted both the cashier and the young mother to know that it wasn't a problem for him to have to wait. He reached into the cooler and pulled out three different ice cream novelties and waited his turn. He hoped he got out of the store quick enough to catch the woman before she got too far away. He wasn't sure if she had walked or driven to the store. If she had walked it would be easy to find her, if she got in a car, she might be gone before he could make his offer of a cold treat.

After he paid, he went to the parking lot quickly to look for the woman and the young girl. He had lucked out, they did have a car, but the child had to be put into a car seat so it was taking them some time to be ready to pull away. He approached her but didn't get too close before he said, "I'm hoping you can help me out."

The woman looked at him and although she didn't look afraid of him, she was definitely puzzled as to what he was hoping to get from her. "In what way?" she asked skeptically.

"I have a horrible sweet tooth, and I tend to impulse buy when I see something I love as much as I love ice cream." Ray began. "The thing is, I'm headed out to take pictures of the canyon all day and all I have is a cooler with a small bag of ice. These are going to be a puddle before I have a chance to eat them with a day as hot as this one is. I was wondering if you would by any chance be interested in helping me out by taking one each. I'm sure I can eat one before it melts, but I don't think I should try for three or I'll be sick to my stomach and not get my photos taken."

The woman looked at him like she thought he was crazy, but from the back seat, the young girl said, "Can we mommy? Can we have ice cream, please?"

"It really would be doing me a favor." Ray stated.

The woman short of shook her head and shrugged her shoulders. She obviously didn't believe Ray at all, but she had a daughter that really wanted ice cream. It was only mid-morning and already the day was proving to be really hot. "Okay." she said reluctantly. "Sure, we'll take ice cream."

"Yay!" the young girl exclaimed.

Ray walked closer and said, "Take your pick, I really like them all." He held out the three packages for the woman to choose.

"I want chocolate, mommy!"

"I know Maggie." the young mother said. Then she looked at Ray as if she had just realized that she probably shouldn't be giving too much information to a complete stranger.

Ray handed her the chocolate one to give to her daughter and then said "I'm Ray Hawthorne. I'm originally from LA, but I'm traveling around the country taking photos for travel magazines and the like."

When she had given the unwrapped treat to her daughter, she turned back to Ray and said, "Nice to meet you, I'm Heidi." She reached for the strawberry treat and began unwrapping it. "I really appreciate this; things have been a little tight lately and buying treats just hasn't been an option. I feel bad that I can't do those things for Maggie."

"I know every parent wants to give treats to their children, but trust me, it means far more to her to have your unconditional love and your care. My dad left when I was a kid, and my mom didn't always have a lot of money, but I always knew she loved me. That meant far more than a bit of ice cream would have."

"I appreciate that." Heidi said. "My husband died six months ago and we're still waiting to see if there is going to be a settlement."

"I don't mean to pry, but if you are waiting for a settlement, I'm assuming that means there is some sort of legal battle or insurance battle going on. You don't have to tell me what it is, that's none of my business, but do you have a good attorney?" Ray asked.

"We don't have many good attorneys around here." Heidi said. "Small towns take what they can get. I have an attorney, yes."

"I have a friend that may be able to help you find someone that would be more helpful. If you don't mind giving me your contact information, I can have her get in touch and at least discuss things. She may not be able to help, but it can't hurt to at least talk to her." Ray offered.

"Okay, yeah, sure." Heidi said. Afterall, he was only asking for her number, he wasn't getting her address. Sure, if he were some sort of a stalker, he could figure out a way to track her down using her phone number, but he didn't give off that type of a vibe to her. After all, he had bought ice cream for a four year old. She gave him her number and they said their goodbyes.

Ray made sure everything was in the cooler with the ice and then he went back into the store. "Is there a manager here that I could speak to by any chance?" he asked the kid behind the counter.

The kid looked a little nervous about that question, but he called the manager from the office. "Can I help you, sir?" the woman asked.

"I hope so." Ray said. "There was a young woman with a child that was just in here, Heidi. Do you know her?"

The manager seemed a little hesitant to say much but the fact that Ray had known her name helped a little. "I've seen her in here." she said hesitantly.

"I'd like to by fifty ice creams for her and her little girl Maggie." Ray said. "I want them to be able to have one whenever they come in until the money runs out. Can you arrange that for me?"

"Uh, yes, sure, we can set that up." the manager stated. "I've never done it before, but I'm sure we can do something."

Ray noticed a display of prepaid cards for sale and said, "How about we calculate how much that will cost and I buy one of these prepaid debit cards for that amount. I'll add a little extra to allow for price fluctuations and then if it buys more than fifty, so be it."

"That would work." the manager said. "I'll make sure my staff knows."

Ray and the manager worked out approximately how much the ice cream would cost, and Ray rounded up by quite a bit and said that if they were ever short for milk or anything else, to take it out of that money. He made his way back out to his car and headed up towards the canyon.

When he was outside of the small town, he hit the speaker button for his phone to work through the radio.

When the woman picked up on the other end, she said, "Well, Ray Hawthorne. To what do I owe the privilege, I hear you're out seeing the countryside."

"That I am," Ray began. "How have you been Kate?"

"I've been good." the woman said. "What can I do for you?"

"Well, I just met this woman, and I'll be honest, I don't really know her at all, but she mentioned something about waiting a long time to hear about some settlement in her husband's death. She's trying to raise a small child and I get the feeling that it's a real struggle. I know you can't actually represent her, I'm in Arizona now, but I was wondering if you'd at least be willing to give her a call and hear her out and see if you have any pointers or input for her."

"I'd be glad to give her a call and at least make sure she's getting the right type of representation." Kate said.

"Great, I'll text you her number when I get to my next stop." Ray said. "I really appreciate this, Kate. Like I said, I don't know her, but she wasn't able to buy her daughter ice cream at the store today because things were tight for her and if there's a pot of money sitting out there that should be hers, I'd like to see her be able to get it."

"Let me guess, you bought them both ice cream." Kate said with a smile in her voice.

"I did." Ray admitted.

"That's the Ray Hawthorne we all know and love." she said. "I miss having you in town, I don't see you at any of the usual spots, but I'm happy to hear that you're out there paying it forward like you always have."

"Thanks, Kate." Ray said. "I guess it's just always been a part of me. I've always tried to take care of the underdog."

"I know, Ray." Kate said. "I was on the receiving end of your kindness often in school. I've always appreciated everything you did for me to help me when we were kids."

"Hey, you were the one that didn't mind hanging out with the guy that everyone thought was some kind of a do-gooder religious fanatic." Ray chuckled.

"The only kids that thought that were the ones that were too rich and too cool to ever think they needed help from anyone, ever." Kate said. "Everyone that was an underdog loved having you around."

"Yeah, well, maybe." Ray said. "I should let you go, I'm getting close to where I want to stop for my first set of photos for the day. I'll send you that text shortly."

"I'll be watching for it." Kate said and then disconnected the call.

Ray found the public parking area that was his first planned stop for the day and pulled in. He sent off a quick text to Kate and another one to Heidi to let her know that Kate would be calling her sometime soon. Before he had all of his equipment unloaded, both women and sent him a 'thank you'.

He took photos for a while but decided he needed to grab lunch somewhere. He pulled up the map on his phone to find a local diner or something. He realized that during his entire trip, the thing he had used his GPS for most often was to find food. He had used it a couple of times to find a specific location on the canyon, but otherwise, he hadn't really used it much. And that was just how he intended for his entire trip to be. GPS only when he needed to find a specific location. Otherwise, he would just follow his instinct and find what was out there.

He had stayed until the sun was almost gone taking photos of the canyon. This was a different location than he had gone to before, but the sun on the canyon walls had just been too beautiful to ignore. He used his phone again to find the nearest hotel with vacancy and headed there for the night.

Another long day of taking photographs from a couple of locations had him debating if he should drive back to Dick's or if he should just stay in the hotel another night. He called Beth to see how things were going to see if he could maybe get a read on what she thought might be best. She had informed him that Dick was hoping to invite the whole family over for a cookout whenever Ray got back. She suggested that maybe Dick felt like Ray knew Danielle better than any of them did and it might be best if he were there.

"Go ahead and set it up for tomorrow, late afternoon or evening if that works for you." Ray suggested. "I'll spend the night here but get an early start in the morning, I'm not much more than an hour away. Do you want me to call Danielle, or are you planning to do it?"

"I'll call her, it's time I start getting to know my niece." Beth stated. "I'll send a text after I talk to her to let you know for sure if we're on for tomorrow and what time."

"Sounds good." Ray said. "I'll see you sometime tomorrow either way. How's your dad doing?"

"He's been pretty quiet." Beth said with concern. "We've tried to be around, and have the kids around, hoping maybe it would give him a boost, but it hasn't gone over really well."

"That's to be expected I suppose." Ray said. "Sixty-seven years is a long time."

"I know." Beth agreed, it's just hard to think that we might lose him too."

Ray didn't really have anything more to say to that, and really, neither did Beth. They both knew that there was a possibility that Dick would just give up now that he didn't have Millie to focus on and care for.

Chapter Ten

Ray had gotten a text from Beth telling him what time the cookout was planned for, and he had asked if there were anything they wanted him to pick up on his way back. She had told him they had it covered so he took a few more photos and then headed to Dick's house. He got there in time to take care of his things before Danielle arrived.

His phone dinged with a text. Heidi had sent a photo of Maggie after she had eaten her ice cream with a message saying. "Your friend called, thank you. I thought you might like this picture." Her lips were surrounded by the chocolate, but the smile on her face told the whole story of how much she had enjoyed the treat. Ray saved the photo to his phone and sent a "thank you" to Heidi. He found that most often, the landmarks were recorded on his camera, but the people where on his phone. They wouldn't go to a magazine or travel brochure, but he would cherish the ones on his phone because each one brought a memory to mind. He had taken photos of everyone he had made connections with in Thousand Palms. He had already taken some of Dick and Millie and their family. He would add the one of Maggie to that folder and look back at them often. This trip and the people he was meeting along the way were going to be something he wanted to remember for years to come. He didn't know how long it would take him to travel the country, but he supposed that at some point in time, he would have seen everything he wanted to see, and he would pick a place to settle down and live out the rest of his life. He might find himself back in LA or he might find a city that he fell in love with and end up calling it home.

He had just gotten his things all put away and was coming back downstairs when Danielle arrived. He greeted her and showed her the way to the backyard where everyone else was already gathered. He introduced her to Tom but let Beth handle the rest of the introductions. He had met her children and grandchildren, but he wasn't sure he remembered all of the names correctly. Rather than take a chance of messing it up, he just stepped aside and let Beth handle it.

He walked over to where Dick was sitting in a lawn chair in the shade. "How are you doing, Dick?"

"I just don't know that I know which way is up anymore, Ray." Dick said sadly. "I feel like my whole world turned topsy turvy."

"I can understand that." Ray said. "You lost your companion and you found your granddaughter you weren't sure you even had.

"She's a beautiful girl, isn't she?" Dick said.

"Yes, she is." Ray agreed.

"She reminds me a lot of my Millie when she was young. She looks exactly like Daniel, but she has a lot of the similar features as Mille did when she was young." Dick said.

"What happened between you and Daniel that caused you to not know about Danielle?" Ray asked. Then he realized that it may be too personal and added, "If you don't want to tell me that's fine. I know I'm not family."

"No, it's a fair question." Dick said. He paused as if he were trying to find the right words. "I know they say not to speak ill of the dead, but the last few years of his life, Daniel turned against everything we had taught him growing up. He didn't want to have anything to do with church. He wanted to drink and party more than much of anything else. He wasn't really holding down any sort of a decent job and I had heard rumors that he had gotten someone pregnant, although I never knew who. I confronted him one night and asked him if that were true. I told him that I had taught him better than that and that I expected him to at least step up and help with the child. I told him that even if he didn't want to be with the mother long term, he owed it to that child to make sure it was provided for."

"Did he admit to having a child?" Ray asked.

"Not in so many words." Dick said. "He sidestepped that issue. He said that he wasn't ready for kids, that he didn't have a single woman in his life, he liked playing the field and dating more than one. So, I wasn't sure if he was saying that he didn't have a child or if he was just saying that it didn't matter to him if he did or not."

"So, you suspected it, but weren't sure until Danielle walked into the funeral home?" Ray asked.

"No, I was pretty sure long before that." Dick said. "Like I told you, my Millie was a whiz with money, and I didn't know what most of it was going to, but every once in a while, I'd see something that made me think she was buying things for a little girl. Not that it would have been completely odd because of Beth's children, but it never seemed to match up age or size wise when I did see something. Looking back, I should have confronted Millie about it long ago, but I guess it was easier to bury my head in the sand. If the child did exist, what did that say about my son? If I had known for sure, it would have been even harder to not hold Daniel responsible and confront him again. I think it was a situation of I knew, but I didn't want to know, so I didn't admit it to myself. I wish I had done things differently now, but I can't go back and fix any of it."

"They always say hindsight is twenty/twenty." Ray said. "But you have a chance now to get to know your granddaughter."

"We all do." Beth said as she walked up to them. "Just checking to see if everything's okay. Food should be ready in about ten minutes. Danielle and I are going to go in and finish up the salads and fruit."

When the two women went inside, and Danielle began talking. "I overheard your dad say some things about my dad."

"I know, your grandpa doesn't exactly talk softly." Beth said. "Don't let anything he says hurt you though. Your dad had some struggles in the last few years of his life, but when we were growing up, he was a great big brother. He used to take me to the county fair and win me all sorts of stuffed animals and things. He was enough older that by the time I was in third or fourth grade, he could drive. He never denied me going with him to things like that. Oh, if he had a date, I didn't get to go. But he always made sure he took me to the fair on one of the days it was open. He'd take me to the penny carnival at school too. He was a good big brother when we were growing up. It was after he grew up and went out on his own that I think he got in with the wrong sort of friends. It was like he was a really good person, and then all of a sudden, he wasn't. I don't really know what happened. I was eight years younger than he was, so I'm sure my parents kept some of it from me. We were raised going to church, every time the doors were open, we were there. I don't know if he just got tired of the religious aspects and turned his back on it because it had been forced on us, or if he just got in with the wrong type of people. I don't know exactly what was said or if anything was done, but I did know that my dad had a falling out with my brother on more than one occasion. I think maybe my dad was trying to get Daniel to get back into going to church, and my he's never been anything less than vocal about his belief that everyone should attend church regularly. In the last few years, his own attendance has suffered because he just didn't get out much other than to go and see my mom. I'm sure that's part of what made him not go to church too. He wanted to go to the nursing home every day and two outings has been too much for him for a while now. But twenty years ago, if the church was having a meeting, he was there. It didn't matter if there was some crusade or something going on that took up every night of the week. My dad was there sitting in his normal pew. He was a board member and taught Sunday school and all of that. He was the song leader for years. Church was the most important thing in his life. Sometimes I wondered if he loved the church more than anything except family. And I guess I even wondered if when Daniel turned his back on the church if that was what made my dad kind of disown him. I could be way off base, like I said, they hid a lot of it from me so I don't know what went wrong. I just knew that Daniel stopped coming around and that seemed to bother my mom a lot more than it did my dad. But the one thing that I can promise you is that anything your dad may or may not have done, my dad won't hold that against you. He's not that type of person. You walked in with a clean slate and he'll give you every opportunity to be a part of the family if you want to. I think at some point, he'll want to hear your stories about the things mom did with you too. It may be a little too raw right now, but eventually, he'll want those stories too."

"I can do that, whenever he's ready." Danielle said. "She was a really great person. I'm glad I had her in my life. When my mom died, she was really the only one I had left. At least the only one that I had met. My mom had cousins and stuff, but I never really knew them."

"Well, you have a family now. We all want to get to know you." Beth said. "I don't want to frighten you off, but would it be okay if I gave you a hug?"

"That would be great." Danielle said.

While they had been talking, they had finished getting the fruit onto the tray and the salad fixings out of the fridge. They carried the fruit and vegetables out to the back porch where the rest of the food was set up and Beth called everyone to come and fix a plate. "I'll make one for you if you want me to dad."

"That would be fine." Dick said.

When Beth had the plate ready, Danielle asked, "Can I take it to him?"

"Sure." Beth agreed handing her the plate.

Danielle walked over and handed him the plate. She sat beside him and said, "I know you probably aren't ready to hear them, but sometime I'd like to share some of my memories of my grandma with you."

"I'd love to hear them now." Dick said.

Danielle looked at him and though there was a sadness there, she could see that he kind of needed to hear these things. She took a deep breath and began. "I think I was maybe three when I remember seeing her for the first time. I was at the park with my mom and there was this lady sitting on the bench. They were talking for a while and I just kept playing. After a while, my mom called me over and introduced me. She didn't say Millie was my grandmother. I think maybe they had decided that I was too young to really comprehend it all, so she just told me the lady was named Millie and that she wanted to be our friend. I was fine with that, I always loved people."

"That was something you have in common with her then." Dick said. "My Millie always loved people. Even in her last few years, nothing made her happier than having someone come to visit."

"I remember seeing her a lot, probably at least once a month." Danielle continued. "Sometimes at the park, she'd get me an ice cream. I remember seeing her at the library too. I'd be there for story time or whatever and she'd come over after they were done reading and we'd talk about my favorite books. She'd read me one from my favorite author. She used to make it fun with noises. Like if there was a bird chirping in the story, she would make a 'chirp, chirp' sound. I loved listening to her read me a story."

"She loved children and her mother had always taught her the value of books." Dick said.

"She passed that on to me then." Danielle said. "I always cherished books, so much so that I work at the library now. I think some of my best memories were in that old Victorian house that the library was in when I was a child. It was a magical place. My grandma made sure of it with the voices and the books that she always shared with me. When they opened the new building, I think it hurt her heart as much as it did mine that we didn't get to go to that building anymore. The new one was nice, with all the modern things, but that old house just held so many memories. I know some people would think it was strange, but Grandma agreed with me that it smelled like books when you walked in there. At least that was the smell that I associated as books. I'm sure it was partially the building and it's age, but there was just a certain smell when you walked in and in my mind that was a scent called books."

Dick gave her a smile and she wasn't sure if he was thinking that was sweet or if he was thinking it was a little crazy, but that didn't matter, she continued on with her story. "I remember the first time I walked into the new building with her. I wrinkled up my nose because the smell just wasn't there. She looked and me and she nodded. She said 'I know, it doesn't smell like books yet, does it?'. I just shook my head and she said 'maybe someday it will, but probably not for a long, long time.' We were both sad that it wasn't the same anymore."

She paused to think about what else to tell him. "I remember I had checked out my usual five books for the week, and a little boy that my mom babysat sometimes got ahold of a black marker and scribbled all over every single page. It devastated me to see someone do that to a book. I showed it to Millie and I think that was the first time she said anything about being my grandma. She told me that it was horrible what that boy had done, but she was going to go to the library and make sure that they had enough money to buy a brand new book to replace it. She said something like 'grandma will make it right' or something similar. I still didn't really think that she was actually my grandma. I knew my mom's parents. I just thought that Millie was kind of like the grandmotherly type. You know, like a woman who just loves every little kid and so she's a grandma to everyone. I think I was in second or third grade when I finally figured out that she actually was my real grandma. We had to write a story about our family, and I asked my mom if I should include Millie. She said 'why not, she's your grandma'. I still didn't fully understand, but my mom explained to me that I had a dad and by that time he had died, but Millie was his mom, so yes, she was actually my grandma."

"Did you know your father at all?" Dick asked.

"I remember him sort of." Danielle said. "I know he came around sometimes. He didn't really stay with us for long, but I was only three when he died, so my memories are kind of hard to define. I remember him, but I also know I was told a lot about him as I grew up so some of it may be actual memories and some of it may be mixed with the stories I was told."

"I'm sorry he didn't try harder to be a part of your life." Dick said sadly. "That may be partially my fault. I always pushed him so hard that he may have rebelled against it because he knew it was what I wanted him to do."

"That's not on you, Grandpa." Danielle said. "That's on him." It was then that she realized what she had just called him. "I'm sorry, that just sort of slipped out. If you aren't okay with me calling you grandpa, I can refrain from it in the future."

"Why would I mind, child? It's what I am." Dick said. "It's going to take some time for both of us to work out what we want and need from each other or if we want to keep it more distant, but it's a fact of life that you are my granddaughter and it's perfectly fine for you to call me your grandfather."

"I know it's not something that you probably want the whole town to know about. It would probably bring up a lot of questions." Danielle began.

Dick interrupted her. "Nonsense! I don't care who knows. I've lived in the town for over fifty years. If they want to think different about me after finding out about you than they did before they found out, I couldn't care less. I've not got too many more days on this earth, I don't have anyone to impress at this point."

"Don't say that, Grandpa." Danielle said. "I had years to get to know Grandma, I need to have time to get to know you too."

"Well, I'm ninety-one years old, Danielle." Dick said. "I don't mean to say that I'm giving up and going to be gone tomorrow, but I have a bad heart and other things that won't let me last forever either."

"I know, but please try to keep yourself healthy." Danielle implored. "I want to get to know you. I'm just asking you to not give up just because Grandma died."

Dick didn't really respond to her so they both munched on their food for a while.

Danielle didn't want to leave him to dwell on his own mortality for long though, so she started with her stories again. "I remember every year, Grandma would pick my mom and I up and we'd go into the city to buy school clothes and supplies. My mom didn't have a lot of money, but she still paid for what she could. Grandma always let me pick out the backpack and notebook and everything that I wanted and she'd get a few more outfits than what my mom could buy. She always made sure that I had an outfit for the first day of school too. I got to pick out whatever I wanted for that first day. Kids always want to dress to impress on that first day I guess. It's kind of like wanting to make a good first impression. The kids that walk in with old clothes are immediately labeled as the poor kids. The ones that walk in with new clothes from Walmart are labeled as the sort of middle of the road, and the ones that walked in with clothes from the mall were the upper echelon I guess. I don't know why that's a thing even in elementary school, but it is and Grandma always made sure I had the things that would make a good first impression. She didn't buy me stuff from the really rich stores, but it was still always a step above Walmart."

"She had a big heart." Dick said.

"Yes, she did." Danielle agreed. "There were always things under the Christmas tree from Santa and a stocking full of treats and small toys. After I got old enough to not believe in Santa anymore, I figured out that it had always been Grandma that made sure I had that. Up until she started getting sick, I still got presents and a stocking from Santa. One time I sat down and told her that I was too old to believe in Santa anymore and that I knew it was her. She kind of scolded me for that, oh not in a mean way, but she told me that no one was ever too old to believe in Santa Claus. Everyone should remember that Santa isn't a person, he's more of a spirt of good will and giving. She said that anyone that wanted to give a gift without wanting or needing any acknowledgement of the fact that they had given it, was Santa."

"She always was that way." Dick said. "Even when our kids and grandchildren got old enough that it didn't really matter to them, it mattered to her. They always had a gift of some sort that didn't come from us, it came from Santa. It was her spirit of love and giving that made her so special."

"It was." Danielle agreed. "When she first went into the nursing home, I tried to go and see her, but I was cautious because I didn't want her to have to tell you who I was. I often went right after vising hours started or just before they ended. When she got closer to the end, she didn't always know who I was, but I went and sat with her anyway. We talked about things, most of them were just nonsense, but she always told me that she had a husband who loved her so much. She asked me if

I had ever met her husband. I didn't remind her that she was the one that had asked me to not say anything to you. She wasn't sure how you would feel about me being Daniel's daughter and she wasn't sure how you would feel about what she did for me as I grew up. She told me that you wouldn't have had a problem with her spending money on me and things because you always let her spend how she saw fit. She did worry though that if you hadn't forgiven my dad for what he had done that you would have a hard time accepting me."

"I can't really say what I would have done or how I would have felt." Dick admitted. "I would like to think that I would have embraced having a granddaughter, but I did have a tough spot when it came to anything to do with your father. I had asked him if he had gotten a woman pregnant, and he wouldn't admit to me if he had or not." Dick was quiet and lost in thought for a few minutes but then he said, "I guess we'll never know what I would have done, all I can say is what I want to do now. I want you to be a part of this family and I want you to be in my life for however much longer I am here."

"I want that too, Grandpa." Danielle said. She leaned over and gave him a tight hug and a kiss on his cheek. "I want to be a part of this whole family, if everyone will let me."

Ray had sat near Dick and Danielle. He was hoping they would do exactly what they had done and talked things out and come to a good place. He hadn't planned to intervene unless something hurtful had been said by one or the other. He was happy that he hadn't had to chime in at all. It seemed like they were off to a good start and for the most part, the future, however long it would last would be a time for them to work on making up for lost time. Oh, Ray knew you could never go back and make up for the past. Danielle was twenty-three, they couldn't go back, but they could move forward in a positive direction.

That also made him realize that he needed to follow his own path towards making a future and not trying to make up for his past. It was time that he did more than just know where his half-brother lived. It was time to try to contact him and start working on a line of communication that would hopefully start to build a bridge that he could cross and they could meet someday. He knew where the man lived, it wasn't all that many states away. He also didn't want to just show up on his doorstep and announce himself as the long lost half-brother. If Ray were to be honest, he had no idea if the man even knew he existed. He wasn't sure what if anything their father had told his new family about his old one. He stepped away from the group and picked up his phone. When the man on the other end answered, Ray said, "Hey. I'm wondering if you can find out an address or a phone number for me. I'm trying to track down my half-brother. I know what city he lives in but I'm not sure of an address."

"You do know that most of that can be found on the Internet now, right Ray?" his old friend said with a chuckle. "The days of having to hire a PI to track someone down are long gone. Hell, try Facebook, almost everyone under the age of sixty is on there, and many that are over sixty are too. If you don't find him, let me know, but I'll bet if you use any legitimate search engine, and put in his name and his city, you'll find him."

"Okay, yeah." Ray agreed. "I guess I'm still somewhat old fashioned, but I'll give it a try. Thanks." He hung up the phone and pulled up the Internet. He put in the name, Patrick Hawthorne and the city in Louisiana he had been told his father had moved to and an address came up. There were also lots of ways to pay for a background check and any other information he might want to obtain. He didn't want to go that route though. He wanted to let his brother tell him who he was, not some paid for piece of paper, although it probably didn't actually get sent to you in paper form. Still, he wanted to know the person, not the report. He opened his social media and sent a friend request. He wasn't sure if the man would accept it or not, but he hoped that having the same last name might help. Now, he just had to wait to see if the man wanted to connect.

Epilogue

Ray felt both sadness and happiness as he drove away from Dick's home. He hadn't really known Millie that long, but he was still saddened by her passing. Even though he wasn't her son, she had believed for the last few weeks that he was. And therefore, he had tried really hard to be like a son to her in many ways. He had never called her mom, but he had never called her Millie either. He let her believe that her son was there in her final days. He had often kissed her on the top of the head when he told her goodbye at the end of a visit. But now, Millie was in heaven or wherever one believed good souls went at the end of their life. She wasn't in pain or struggling to eat her food. She wasn't confused or feeling alone anymore.

Dick had lost his wife, but he had regained his daughter and added a new granddaughter. One that he had never really known he had. The tension that had built over things none of them could control was in the past and Dick and Beth were close again. And a bond was being built between all of them and Danielle. Ray wasn't sure how much longer Dick would be on this earth, because everyone had seen the beginning of his decline in health the minute Millie had passed. It was as if he had forced himself to keep going so that Millie had someone there to comfort her in the end, but now that she was gone, he had no reason to stay anymore. Even though he had said that he wanted to go first, Ray could tell that there was a part of him that had kept going so that Millie wasn't alone in her final days. Some might argue that his daughter was a reason to fight, others would believe that he might want to have time to get to know the new found member of the family, but even Beth had told him that she knew he was anxious to see his Millie again someday.

Ray was sad that Millie was gone, but he was glad that he had gotten a chance to know her and her family and that he had been even a small part in her last days being happy ones.

He headed on down the road, as usual, he had a direction in mind, but he didn't have specific path to get there. He was just going to head east, wherever east led him.

It turned out that east led him to a small town in Texas where he had to stop for gas. It was definitely one of those places that people referred to as a sleepy little town. He hadn't seen a population sign, but the number couldn't have been very high. He was a little surprised that it had more than a gas station and a grocery store, but it also appeared to have a business that seemed to be a lumber yard and a farm store all in one. That kind of made sense though, because the roads he had been driving down seemed to mostly have farms or ranches. Ray had never really been sure what the difference was they both tended to have animals and crops. Oh well, ranch or farm, it would make sense that a small town would have one store that catered to that unlike bigger towns where they were more likely to be separate.

While he was pumping his gas, he had heard a ding on his phone. He pulled it out to check his notifications and was happy to see that there was a notification from Facebook that Patrick had accepted his friend request. Part of him wanted to message the man immediately and try to connect, but the gas was done pumping and he didn't want to seem like he was pouncing on the man. He would start watching for posts and photos and make sure to post some things of his own so that his half-brother could get to know him a little bit if he actually checked his social media very much. He tucked his phone back away and went in to pay for his gas.

He pulled out of the gas station and was driving down the only main road in town when a small boy on a bike swerved almost in front of him. It appeared the boy had a couple of bags of groceries he was trying to balance while also trying to keep the bike upright. Ray had been able to stop in time, but it apparently still startled the boy because he tipped over on his bike and food went scattering.

Ray pulled far enough ahead that he wouldn't scare the kid again before pulling off the side of the road. He shut off the car and went to make sure the kid was okay. "Hey, are you alright?"

"Yeah, I'm okay, I just spilled everything, it's hard to balance it on a bike." the boy said. "But I'll get it figured out, my mom needs me to get this stuff home. She's got to have this stuff before time for dinner."

"I'm sure it will be okay." Ray said, helping the boy pick up the things that had scattered. "Do you think your mom would mind if I gave you a ride home with all of this stuff? I'm Ray." He held out his hand and the young boy shook it.

"I'm Christopher." the boy said. He thought about it for a minute and said, "I think it might be okay."

Ray helped him get the bike and the groceries into the SUV and then told him to buckle up. The boy gave directions on how to get to his house. As they pulled up, Ray could see several places where the fence was in desperate need of repair. When they pulled into the driveway, he saw a redheaded woman carrying a bale of hay into the barn. She wasn't really struggling with it, but it was obvious that it wasn't an easy task either. Ray wondered if she had a husband and if so, why he wasn't lifting the heavy bales.

"Is that your mom?" Ray asked, nodding toward the woman.

"Yep, that's her." the boy said with obvious pride.

"Is your dad around anywhere?"

The boy's smile faded a little and Ray was sure he was going to say that there was no dad, instead he said "Yeah, he's in the house, but he's been kind of sick."

Afterword

While the characters Dick and Millie are fictitious, many of the characteristics that Millie exhibits are based on my own mother. In November of 2020 she was diagnosed with moderate to severe Alzheimer's. She had begun to do things like put pancake batter on the table without cooking it. She had read the recipe and had made the batter according to the directions, however they said nothing about how to cook it, so she thought she was done. She had ruined a new microwave by putting tin foil into it. We noticed things more and more as time went by. But at the end of January 2021, she fell and broke her hip. She had to have a titanium rod put in and she spent three days in the hospital. However, she also had to spend three weeks in rehab. This was during the time when no one was allowed to visit patients in hospitals or nursing homes because of COVID. She spent three weeks not seeing anyone she knew and loved. I sincerely believe that made her condition deteriorate quickly.

By the time she came home, she really only recognized my dad every time. Sometimes she knew who other people were, sometimes she didn't. In the year since then, she has gotten to the point where the only person she knows for sure is my father. She has made the statement that Millie makes in the book that she doesn't have a daughter. That was a hard thing to hear, but I have had to remind myself that it is the disease and not her real thoughts. We have been able to keep from putting my mom in a home, so far at least. My father is 91 with congestive heart failure and he is unable to do all the cooking and other things around the house, so my husband and I have moved in with him to help with meals and taking care of both of their medical situations.

I've learned a lot about this disease in the last year or so. I've studied it so that I would know what to expect. It's true that the taste buds change and things that they used to love are no longer flavorful to them anymore. Most nights, no matter what I make for dinner it "has no flavor" or "I don't like it" is heard from my mom. At first, that bothered me, and I wanted to try harder to make something she would like. I've resolved myself to the fact that it's not me, and it's not her, it's her disease. The best I can do is try to provide the calories she needs for her body to keep going. If she turns down beef stew for a peanut butter and jelly sandwich, well that's okay, at least she's eating something. The one thing that she still loves is anything sweet. So, we have to keep those things out of sight until she's eaten something with at least a little substance to it.

It's something I never thought would hit her of all people. My grandmother was completely with it mentally until she went into the hospital and was gone within a couple of days. No one else in my mom's family has had this disease to my knowledge and my mom was always great with money and finances. She used to do bookkeeping for businesses in our small town. She no longer understands the concept of money. She knows what it is when she sees it, but the concept of what it is and what it does is gone for her.

This book was difficult to write, because it hits so close to home, but I felt that it was a story that needed telling and if I can raise any awareness for Alzheimer's either through this story or through the proceeds it raises being donated to the charity, then I have done something that needed to be done.

Thanks for reading my story.

Also By Riley Dawson

Backroads Benefactor Series:
Road to Redemption Available now
Road to Rebuilding Coming July 2022

Made in the USA
Columbia, SC
15 July 2022

63483452R00100